DEAD POETS DON'T BLEED

By

Barbara J. Less

ISBN: 0-7596-5929-X

This book is printed on acid free paper.

1stBooks - rev. 8/29/01

PROLOGUE

"Hey, look there's a beached whale here!" cried a boy in a wet suit.

"The tide must have dragged him in." His companion crept closer to the dune. His mouth drooped in disappointment. "Nah, it's only a man, all bloated up."

"Do you think he's dead?" the first boy asked.

"Let me see?" The second boy jabbed the man's stomach with a corner of his green surf board. "He don't move or nothin"

"Put somethin' heavy on him, Mikey, so he don't drift back into the ocean. Are there any rocks around?"

"No, just clam shells."

Foam from the incoming tide splashed against the boy's ankles. The body slid a few feet toward the water.

Shoving his surfboard between the man's hairy legs, Mikey stepped back. "There, that should anchor him."

"Yeah, good thinking, Mikey."

"Hey, what have you got there?" A white-haired man waving a cane hobbled over. His mouth gaped open. "That's Charlie Masterson. I'd recognize him anywhere." Crouching to get a better look, he pointed to the man's chest. "Those look like bullet holes."

"Hey mister," the boy named Mikey said. "Why don't you put your cane where my surfboard is, so he won't get pulled into the ocean. I need my board." The man nodded and shoved his cane into the damp sand. "Have you boys called the police?"

There was no answer. Looking up, he heard shouts and laughter as the boys sprinted toward the ocean. Watching them, he shook his head. "Kids, nowadays." Let's see there was a pay phone in front of that taco place.

Limping away, he turned to check the body. A sea gull perched on top of his cane.

He scowled, wagging a finger at the gull. “Hey, bird don’t peck at the wood. That cane’s expensive.”

The story made banner headlines in the San Francisco Daily.

WELL-KNOWN NIGHT CLUB OWNER FOUND DEAD ON BEACH.

Detective Dusty Merkel rubbed his thinning red hair, “It’s anybody’s guess who killed him. Yeah Charlie Masterson would never win a popularity contest. But, I’m gonna’ find his killer no matter how long it takes.”

A few weeks later, in the obituaries, a small paragraph mentioned a memorial service for Charlie given by his bereaved widow, Bunnie Masterson.

- 1 -

(Bunnie Masterson)

Bunnie Masterson squashed a cigarette in the ashtray.

Heartly, sprawled on the velvet ottoman, watched. His white tail wagged as she spoke. "Do you realize, Heartly, it's two years since Charlie died. Time sure flies when you're having fun." She inserted her contacts, turning her pale eyes to a rich green. Now where is my poem? She picked up a sheet of pink stationery on the night stand.

Standing, in front of the ottoman, she read. "Passion and ecstasy emerges from my body steamily." She paused. "Well what do yah think of my poem, pup?" If only I could write a second line. Let's see, she grabbed a ball point. "Embracing you with lusty passion." She shook her head. "Damn, they're two 'passions.' Gotta think of another sensual word. Maybe reciting the alphabet will help? "A, B, C," she started. "Oh hell," my mind's a blank, I'll finish it next week. Gray gets so annoyed if we're late." What am I doing in that group, anyhow? Here I am socializing with four old babes and a gigolo poet. At least I don't fawn all over him like the others._

Heartly stretched, expelling a shrill yawn. Pouncing on the pink velvet cushion next to him, she giggled. "You funny boy." She stroked his smooth white fur. "Why can't men be like you, Heartly? Why can't I ever find a man who would act like a well-behaved Italian Greyhound? You're the only good thing Charlie ever gave me." Bunnie reflected; of course, now I own this house in Sea Cliff, plus a few fat bank accounts, but Charlie had to die for me to get them. What a memorial service I gave that louse! I did Charlie proud even if I did have to bribe most of the mourners. Reaching for another cigarette, she thought, better smoke all I can at home, since Gray prohibits them in his fancy condo.

Imagine, he had the gall to put up that "Thank you for not smoking" sign in his living room. She expelled a stream of smoke. You know, Grayson Crown is no different from me, really. We're both supported by dead "Charlies." His renowned father, "Big Time Charlie Crown" pays his rent, and "Good Time Charlie Masterson" pays mine. Yes, I lucked out for a change. Charlie and I stayed married somehow until death did us apart. She grinned, thinking, no divorce court settlements for him. "Poor Charlie," she patted the top of Heartly's head. He should have realized when a broad reaches fifty, she settles down. She has to stop bed-hopping, if only to keep her health, looks and energy.

Funny, when you're finally rid of worry about taking precautions to avoid abortions, the novelty of having different partners loses its appeal.

Heartly jumped on the heart-shaped bed. Peering at the ceiling, he barked a couple of feeble yips.

"Don't be scared, that's just your reflection, pup." Maybe I should take that ceiling mirror down.

Bunnie smiled, watching Heartly bury his small body under the pink comforter.

"Surprise, Charlie, wherever you are," she blurted. "Heartly is sharing your bed with me now. How does that grab you?"

She picked up a corner of the comforter and rubbed the fawn heart-shaped mark on the dog's flank. She whispered, "Charlie claimed an allergy to your fur. Ridiculous, he was just jealous. How dumb did that man think I was? Going so far as to use my blusher on his chest, thinking I'd believe it was a rash."

"Well, gotta' go to my poetry class, pup." She stood before the full-length mirror. Not bad for an old broad. She fluffed her ash-colored ringlets. Still have the same figure as in my modeling days, and if the light isn't too bright, my face still looks pretty good.

She glanced at the watch on her wrist. Good, I'll be early for a change.

Sliding open the closet door, she pulled a black leather jacket off a hanger. The phone rang. I'll just let the machine answer that, she thought. Oh, no, she cringed, hearing Molly whine at the other end. "Bunnie, do I have to wear that leather jacket today?"

She picked up the receiver. "Yes, Molly wear your jacket today."

Every week that woman phones me complaining about our jackets. Those jackets were a brilliant idea. She craned her neck to glimpse the purple letters on the back, "Power of Poetry."

Holding the receiver away from her ear, she let Molly whine, thinking. Most creative thing I've ever designed. Even Grayson thinks so and he's the leader of our group.

"Yes, Molly wear your jacket today," she repeated. "See you at the poetry club. Bye."

Maybe I shouldn't answer the phone on Monday mornings, Bunnie thought, glancing at her diamond studded watch. Good, I'll still be on time.

- 2 -

(Molly Finkel)

Maybe women over sixty shouldn't wear motorcycle jackets. Darn that Bunnie. Molly scrutinized her reflection in the full-length mirror. The black leather did complement her salt and pepper hair.

Twisting, she saw the Gothic lettering on the back, "Power of Poetry." That was a nice word, "Power." She repeated it several times to herself. Power goes with freedom, she thought. I've got them both now. Imagine reading and writing poetry when Seymour was alive. "God rest his soul," she whispered.

Gazing at the sofa, she could still see Seymour sprawled on a faded green pillow. He held a can of beer in one hand and a cigar in the other. The ceramic ashtray on the end table overflowed with cigar butts. She shook her head, remembering, no matter how many times she sprayed air freshner, the stench of those cigars would not go away. His eyes squinted at the football game on the TV screen as he flicked ashes absentmindedly.

Humph! Seymour's legacy, Molly thought. The only thing he left me are those burned holes on the upholstery. "A blessing that he's gone," Molly cringed, instantly wanting to retract her words. Looking up at the ceiling fearfully, she wondered, would God understand? No bolt of lightening flashed. She sighed, nodding, God understands. Besides, she rationalized, who else was there to marry and legalize Leon? _

"You're pregnant with a goy's baby!" Papa yelled. "You come to your senses, Miss, and when Seymour proposed, you accept."

"Such a nice boy, that Seymour," Mama chimed in. Seymour always thought he was Leon's father in spite of the lack of physical resemblance. "Leon takes after Molly's Great Aunt

Rose," Mama explained. "She had the same golden hair and blue eyes."

Evidently Mama's explanation was enough; neither Seymour or Leon ever questioned their relationship. Molly picked up the silver frame on the mantle. She studied the color photograph of Leon. Pepper stood by his shoulder, grinning with those crooked front teeth. Molly shook her head, a handsome boy like Leon could have done better. How fortunate their two little sons in the foreground didn't inherit those teeth. Pepper doesn't discipline the boys at all. Molly scowled, remembering how they tore up the pictures in her family album. Why that Pepper didn't even punish them. She claimed spanking was abusive. "It would stunt their creativity," she explained. That girl and her absurd ideas. "I mean a little tap like I used to give Leon," Molly explained, and look how he turned out. "Leon has problems," Pepper answered.

What problems? Molly wondered. Better not ask her. She'd probably tell me it was due to strict upbringing.

Her eyes misted as she returned the photo to the mantle. Imagine, that daughter-in-law of mine, would let her kids destroy my whole house and never say a word. Instead, she gets angry with me. Maybe it's good they stay in Chicago and don't visit. What a good idea to call Darla Rhodes, the radio advice lady. "Please help me." she pleaded.

Darla told her to release Leon and live her own life. She was right. Never again would she be the nagging mother, or worse, the wicked mother-in-law.

That Darla is an angel, such wisdom she generously shares with anyone who turns on the radio at 4 p.m. every afternoon.

Wiping a tear forming in her eye, Molly wondered. Why didn't Darla warn me of the emptiness I feel not seeing Leon for all these months? Maybe, I should call him tonight?

No, she shook her head, suppressing the urge. Follow Darla's advice, she reminded herself. Now, I finally have a life of my own, new friends and of course, my poems. And, I've gotten to know Nancy, such an educated girl. To think I lived next door all these years and never knew her.

When Seymour and I bought this house in the Sunset District thirty-seven years ago, we were friendly with everyone on the block. The neighborhood's changed, Molly reflected. Today everyone's suspicious of their neighbors.

Molly studied the sheet of binder paper, her latest poem. The one she would recite today. "Wistful Willow Tree," she called it. Perhaps the group would suggest another title. That would be O.K.

They wouldn't like it because it rhymed. I can't write that free verse style like Nancy. Her poetry flows. But, this is my style and they're just gonna' have to accept it. After all they're always talking about poetic license.

The clock chimed. It's time, she thought. Folding her poem, she placed it in her large handbag. Hope I won't have to wait too long for Nancy.

With agility, she stepped over the low picket fence that separated the houses. She walked into the tunnel entrance of the yellow stucco. Before Molly had a chance to ring the doorbell, she spotted Nancy, clad in a blue terry robe, collecting the newspaper.

"I'm sorry, I didn't realize it was so late, Molly. I was finishing my poem. I'll just be a few minutes."

Molly nodded and followed Nancy up the brick steps into the living room. Sitting in a newly upholstered winged chair, she admired the Early American decor. Everything looks so nice. That Nancy is some housekeeper.

- 3 -

(Nancy Franklin)

Nancy Franklin would have enjoyed lingering in the shower longer, but Molly was downstairs waiting. Reluctantly, she turned off the warm spray, grabbed a towel from the chrome holder and began drying herself.

Creating that poem has drained my energy. "The Angler of Eternity," is my finest effort at symbolism. If only I can read it without displaying too much emotion or worse, crying.

Blowing her short brown hair dry, she smiled at her reflection in the bathroom mirror. How pleased Alan would have been at her talent though fishing wasn't one of his favorite sports. Somehow, she had captured him in her verse. Not the skeleton of a creature he became the months before he died, but a young, vibrant Alan. The one she fell in love with during their second year at the University. Alan's eyes glowed with enthusiasm then. He possessed a passion for life that was contagious. "Alan," she whispered, you're the only man I ever loved."

Closing her eyes, she tried to forget the drugs and incessant pain as the tumor grew. Odd how you think you're invincible, but in reality God's creations are so very fragile.

Detailed planning was an important part of the marriage. Perhaps it should have been included as one of the vows. Do you promise to love, honor and schedule everything in your life? That would be unique.

Every carefully planned expectation became a reality, except the one for a family. Two boys and a girl, they both agreed, would be ideal.

After failing for five years to become pregnant, Nancy consulted a physician. Series of tests were inconclusive. Still certain the fault was hers, Nancy consulted a wide range of fertility specialists. She didn't believe the doctors. "There's no reason why you can't have a healthy, normal baby, Mrs. Franklin."

Twelve years later, Alan confessed, "Mumps, I had them when I was fourteen."

For years they desperately tried to adopt an infant. There were promises from agencies, but never enough babies. If only Alan wasn't so stubborn, insisting on an infant.

Sliding open the closet door, she pulled out her tan jump-suit. Hope they don't remember I wore this last week. Now where did I leave my poem?

She peeked in the spare bedroom now her study. Wallpaper with powder blue ducklings for the baby that never occupied the room covered the walls. Nancy spotted the paper next to the computer. I'm lucky to have found the poetry group. After Alan's funeral, visits from family and friends became rare. Lonely hours watching television with a box of tissues by her side was an inadequate diversion.

Tired of depressing soap operas, she turned on the radio one day and discovered Darla Rhodes Advice Show. "You too can get help," the announcer said, repeating a phone number.

Two days later, disguising her voice she pressed the number on her phone. "This is Amelia," she said. It wouldn't do to use my real name, she thought. "I need some advice." Darla's suggestions were helpful. She was instrumental in steering Nancy to the "Power of Poetry" group. Well, not exactly, she had joined a pottery club first. After three days of struggling with a lop-sided jug, Nancy decided to abandon ceramics. Writing poetry is more rewarding than doing pottery, she rationalized. Ironically, Molly Finkel, her next door neighbor, was a member I've lived next to that frumpy little woman for years without realizing how much we have in common.

Oh, dear, I almost forgot about Molly waiting in the living room all this time. "Be right down, Molly." Was Molly wearing her jacket, she wondered? Well, I might as well put mine on.

Bunnie Masterson and her outrageous ideas designing these. She glanced in the mirror. Smiling at her reflection, she murmured, "It's kind of becoming after all." Grabbing the keys for the Buick, she started downstairs. "I'm ready, Molly, sorry you had to wait."

"That's all right." Molly's eyes twinkled. "Do you know who moved in the penthouse right above Grayson?"

"Who?" Nancy asked.

"Darla Rhodes, that's who." "A saint," Nancy responded. "An angel," Molly nodded. Sliding in the passenger side, Molly confided, "I wish I had learned to drive when I was younger."

"You still can, Molly. Why not call up one of those driving schools?

I hear they're pretty good."

"But, you have to be mechanical," Molly protested. "Mechanical, I'm not."

"Me neither, but it has nothing to do with driving."

"Hmmmmm," Molly contemplated. "I'll have to think about it."

"Did you write a poem this week?"

Molly drew out the paper from her purse. "I always manage to write one even if they're not so good. Do you wanna' hear it?"

"Not now, I'll hear it at Grayson's. You know, Molly poetry is wonderful therapy."

"Therapy, who needs therapy?" Molly chuckled.

"Maybe those Strombolli twins?"

- 4 -

(The Stromboli Twins - Flora and Dora)

"We're going to be late if you don't get ready now," Dora Stromboli yelled to her sister. Dora withdrew her head from the corner window of the Victorian.

Flora ignored her twin. She stalked over to the redwood fence carefully avoiding smashing the border of orange marigolds with her gardening boots. Armed with a small carton of iodized salt, she probed the length of the fence. I know there are more of those nasty things out here. Was it possible snails could communicate? Could they possibly tip each other off about her weekly raids, using some sort of sign-language?

Pellets would do a more thorough job, but there was always a possibility the cats would sample the poison. Yes, salt was safer. Besides, it was kind of fun to see them sizzle a few seconds after she sprinkled it on their slimy bodies. She glanced up to see if Dora was still at the bedroom window. I wonder if she's wearing that ridiculous jacket. She looks absurd. I told her she's much too fat to wear something like that. Funny, how we used to wear the same size until she began those eating binges.

My God, I have to watch everything in that refrigerator, so she won't pig out. Our food bills are double what they used to be. What more can I do about her overeating? Why I even phoned the "Advice From Darla Show."

That woman is slick. All she cares about is her ratings. She remembered Darla's words. "Your sister's weight gain as most obsessive eating is due to an emotional problem."

"I'm sick of guarding the refrigerator night and day. What can I do?"

"Nothing," Darla admitted. "She must seek help herself. A self-help group or private counseling would educate her in self-control."

"Fat chance," Flora snapped, grinning at her play on words.

Holding the receiver away from her ear, Flora listened to Darla drone on about obsessive behavior. Gad, the woman must have gone on for a full ten minutes. Probably didn't have any other calls.

A snail, almost hidden by a leaf, stretched an antenna to explore the redwood.

"Got ya!" Flora shouted, shaking a small trickle of salt on the exposed organ.

The guts quickly liquefied. A crisp snapping noise signaled the shell's descent hitting the cement path. Flora watched deriving a secret pleasure from the snail's demise.

Maybe I should write a poem. I could call it Garden Of Death. "A small pinch of salt, seeping ooze spreading fingers of death." she lilted. I bet that would make 'em all sit up and gasp. Would Grayson even dare to critique? Darn it! Should of thought of it before. There's no time to write anything now.

Upstairs, Dora tugged at the leather jacket stubbornly. She would have to wear it open, it wouldn't zip anymore. Tomorrow, I'll get some of that liquid diet food.

Was Flora still out in the garden? She peered at the window, shouting, "Come on in now, Flora. You know Grayson doesn't like it when we're late."

Flora signaled, holding her thumb up.

I hope that means she's coming in.

Earrings, Dora thought, I almost forgot. I wouldn't want to read my poem bare-eared. Her fingers instinctively grasped the black onyx hearts from the jewelry box. Why these? she thought holding them up. Donald had inserted them in a Valentine's card the year before last. She caressed the smooth stones. What would life be like if she had eloped with Donald when he proposed? Sure, he was twenty years her junior, but did that really matter? Why had she hesitated? She'd consulted everyone, even secretly phoning Darla at the radio station. Darla quoted statistics: "Marriages where there is so great an age difference have a 70% chance of not succeeding, even higher if it's a first marriage for one of the partners." Where did she get those percentages, Dora wondered?

"He's after your money," Flora sneered. "Papa worked hard and skimped to provide for us. Now you want to give it all to that fortune hunter."

"Donald loves me."

Flora laughed, "That's funny."

If only I had followed my instincts, not listening to anybody, I would be Mrs. Donald Palmcroft today. Married to my sister, that's what I am now. Dora's deep-amber eyes released a tear. Too many memories with these earrings. I'll wear the silver hoops. Slipping them on, she gazed at her reflection. I'm the pretty one. Flora's features are much coarser. Funny, we were so alike as children. No one could tell us apart. Mama should have given us other names. She thought she was clever introducing us as the Flora Dora girls. Would anyone know now that we are identical twins? Flora strolled into the bedroom. "Where are the cats, they weren't outside?" "Charlotte was sitting in the kitchen earlier. Emily and Lord Byron were sunning themselves by the living room window."

"Okay, just wanted to make sure they're all right. I'm ready, let's go."

"You mean you're not going to change?"

"Why? I haven't a poem to read. Nobody'll care." "At least, wash your face," Dora admonished. "You got a big smudge of dirt on your cheek." Flora disappeared into the bathroom. Dora heard the water running. I feel just like her mother. She's getting so sloppy about her appearance lately, it's embarrassing.

"It's off," Flora grinned. "Let's go."

"Aren't you going to wear your poetry jacket?"

"Not if I can help it. I'll go warm up the Land Rover."

- 5 -

The crystal wine glass fell. An abstract pattern of splattered chardonnay formed on the white carpet.

"Damn!" Grayson exploded.

Retrieving a paper towel from the kitchen, he blotted the stain and poured himself another drink.

Securing the glass in the middle of the marble table, he retreated into the bathroom. He frowned at his reflection in the mirror. I look like hell.

He reached for a small vial from the medicine cabinet. Filling a dropper, he stared at the ceiling as he squeezed two drops into each eye. There, that should take care of the bloodshot appearance. He smoothed the silver hair on his temples. Just enough gray to look distinguished, he thought. Satisfied, he returned to the living room couch.

He gazed out the sliding glass door leading to the balcony. The panoramic view of the Bay Bridge on a clear day was the main reason he purchased the condo. How relaxing to watch those commuters in their eternal rat-race jockeying for position on the wide span. Leaning back on the lemon-colored pillow, he smiled. God must feel this way overlooking us humans from his heavenly throne.

A rumbling above caused the walls to tremble. The portrait of his dead father, Charlie Crown fell, glass shattering. Grayson sat erect. What's she doing now? Doesn't that woman ever quiet down? Every night there's a party up there and during the day, who knows what's happening. What's her secret? How does her voice sound so alert and well-rested on the radio every afternoon?

Ever since that Darla moved in, I haven't had a moment's peace, he grumbled holding the portrait. I've aged ten years in two weeks.

That guy who's staying with her must have a thing for calisthenics, the way the ceiling shakes. Worse than an earthquake. Cupping his chin with a hand, he debated: Should I make another trip up there and tell them to shut up? He pouted, remembering the last time he pushed the gold doorbell to hear the refrain of "Misty." Darla, clad in an electric-blue teddy, leaned against the doorway. The woman had no modesty.

"I'm so sorry, Mr. Crown. We will try to be as quiet as little mice in the future."

She even thanked me for complaining. Well, at least the noise won't interrupt the poetry reading. Grayson checked his watch. She should be leaving for the studio soon. The way those ladies worship Darla, am I sadistic enough to crumble their illusion?

He sipped his wine. I never realized what a drastic effect Mrs. Stoddard's stroke would have on my life. Quiet Mrs. Stoddard, the former owner of the penthouse, resides at Sunny Glades convalescent home, now. Maybe I should send her another bouquet of carnations?

The doorbell chimed. Grayson adjusted his navy blazer before opening the door.

"Hi Gray, I'm early for a change."

"Good afternoon, Bunnie. You're the first, the others should arrive shortly."

Bunnie curled herself on a corner of the couch, watching Grayson bring in a large platter of sandwiches, the bread crust trimmed.

"I've made tuna and chicken today," he announced.

"Have you ever thought of marrying, Gray? You'd make someone a wonderful wife."

Grayson's cheeks flushed. Waving his index finger at her, he warned, "Don't you start with me today," Bunnie. "That racket from above kept me up all night. Darling Darla likes to party. How the hell does she maintain such a pure image?"_

Bunnie snickered. "Good manager, I guess. Some guy by the name of Donald Palmcroft, an exercise nut. He's staying up there." "Donald Palmcroft," Bunnie repeated. So that's where he disappeared to." "You know him?" "A real egotist. You wanna' hear somethin' funny, Gray. That Donald has a tattoo on his chest, a heart with a 'D" in the center. He dates these women with 'D" names and tells 'em he has part of their name next to his heart. What a line!" "I guess he couldn't try it with you, Bunnie." "Nah, there was no way he could turn that tattoo into a 'B.' He finally confessed that the 'D' was for Donald." "Short lived romance, huh?" Grayson grinned. "Poor Dora, that's the one I feel sorry for. That's her Donald, you know. Maybe I should..." The chimes echoed. "Here they come. Just keep your mouth shut, Bunnie. Use some discretion." The Stromboli twins stood in the doorway. "See Dora, we're not late," Flora Stromboli frowned, seeing Bunnie on the couch. Dora ignored her sister. "Hello Grayson, Bunnie. She pulled a paper from her purse and waved it in front of Grayson's face. "I've got my poem ready to read."

"Stupid," Flora muttered under her breath. What am I doing her with these loonies? How I humor that sister of mine.

Grayson dragged the wooden podium to the center of the room. "Now ladies, let's wait for Nancy and Molly before we begin."

"We're here," Molly announced from the doorway.

"Is it true?" Nancy approached Grayson. "Darla Rhodes is living directly above you?"

Grayson half smiled. "It's true."

Molly poked Nancy's elbow. "See, I told yah." She turned toward Grayson. "Do you think she'd give me her autograph?"

Before Grayson could answer, Dora blurted, "Is she as pretty as her photographs?"

"She's pretty," Grayson acknowledged.

"Pretty noisy," Bunnie muttered.

Dora ignored Bunnie's remark. "I hear she's just a little bit of a thing, scarcely five feet tall."

"How wonderful," Molly squealed, "to have a celebrity as your neighbor. You're so lucky, Grayson. You won't even have to call the station for advice. You can walk upstairs whenever you have a problem."

"I do already, Molly."

Bunnie covered her mouth trying to suppress her laughter.

"Ladies, let's begin. I will read one of my poems to open our session."

Placing a blue sheet of paper on the podium, Grayson read: "I celebrate and sing myself, And what I am assume you shall assume For every atom belonging to me as good belongs to you.

I loaf and invite my soul, I lean and loaf at my ease Observing a spear of summer grass.

My tongue, every atom of my blood, Formed from this soil, this air, Born here of parents, born here from parents the same, and their parents the same."

"That sounds familiar." Nancy's brow creased. "Where have I heard that before? Wait, I remember, that's Walt Whitman."

"No my dear," Grayson corrected. "That is Grayson Crown." Molly clasped her hands together," such beautiful words. I don't really understand, but it sounds good."

"Sheer genius," Dora praised.

Flora yawned.

Dora poked her sister, "cover your mouth."

"I still think that's one of Whitman's from The Leaves Of Grass," Nancy insisted.

Bunnie reached for a sandwich. "Well it's Grayson's now, she mumbled, her mouth full of tuna fish.

Raising her hand, Molly pleaded, May I read mine now?"

Grayson escorted her to the podium.

Molly donned rimless glasses which made her dark eyes look twice their size. She cleared her throat. Her voice trembled.

"I call my poem The Wistful Willow Tree, but if any of you can think of a better title it would be all right."

Keeping her eyes focused on the paper, Molly read.

"Weeping teardrops in the stream.

Catching rays of a stars beam.

She stand majestic in God's glory, Symbol of all mankind's glory."

Molly paused, scanning her audience for any reaction. "Shall I go on?"

"Go on, Molly," someone said.

"Oh, wonderful, wistful willow tree, Harboring sorrow the world cannot see.

Sapping grief throughout your root, Bearing tears, your only fruit."

"The end," Molly announced, looking up, her face flushed.

After a few seconds of silence, Nancy and Dora began to clap. "Nice, Molly, very nice."

"Yeah, cute poem," Bunnie joined in.

"May I make one suggestion?" Grayson asked. "Watch your meter, I think it's slightly off."

"But yah like it?" Molly let out an audible sigh, and plopped down on an apricot-colored chair.

"Another suggestion," Grayson leaned back, folding his arms.

Oh, I wish he wouldn't be so critical, Molly thought, looking at him with a hangdog expression. "Yes," she said.

"Have you ever considered transposing your piece to free verse. In my opinion, you were struggling a bit to make it rhyme even using the word glory twice."

Molly lowered her eyes. "That's because I couldn't find another word." Why does he dislike my poetry so much, she thought?

"Can I read mine next?" Dora pleaded. "I call my poem, Purrfectly Wonderful, and it doesn't rhyme, Grayson." Her lips curled in a faint smile, "The title is a play on words since perfectly is spelt with a 'u' and two 'r's'."

Bunnie groaned. "Not another cat poem." God, that's all she writes.

"Say Dora can't you think of anything else?"

Nancy pressed a finger over her mouth. "Shhhhhhh, let her read."

"Thank you, Nancy, I shall begin now."

"Svelte body sleek silhouetted against the window sash, Purring, purring, purring.

Emerald eyes stare at a single sparrow, Purring, purring purring. Sable fur bristles at such a sight."

Hissing, hissing, hissing.

Grayson sneezed. The mere mention of feline fur brought on his allergy.

"God bless you," Molly uttered.

"I'm sorry, but I have to excuse myself, my allergies are acting up."

Flora croaked, grinning at her sister. "You'd think she'd learn.

Everytime she reads one of them cat poems, Grayson's sinuses get congested." She peeled off the bread covering one of the sandwiches.

"Fish or fowl, can't eat either. Oh, hell," she took a bite, "my animal rights group will never know."

"I'm sorry, Grayson," Dora folded her paper. "I won't continue.

Anyway, there's just two more stanzas, and one more 'purring' line." Her eyes misted.

Now she's hurt, thought Flora, happens every week.

"Nancy," Grayson tone was nasal. "Do you have something to share."

"No," Nancy fingered the paper in her purse. It's just too emotional to read. "I started my ceramics class again," she lied. "Been working on a new jug. Didn't have time to write."

"She's such a good poet," Dora whispered to Molly, and her jugs are all lopsided. You'd think she'd realize."

"This session is a bust," Bunnie blared.

"What about you?" Grayson asked. "Do you have a poem to share?"

"Mine's not finished yet, Gray"

"Flora, did you bring a poem today?"

"I'm working on one, Grayson."

"Since no one else has a poem, I have a wonderful idea, ladies. Now I know some of you are having a difficult time writing free verse. I want to show you just how easy it is. We will listen to music, writing anything that pops into our heads."

"Oh dear," Molly moaned.

He turned the stereo on. A flute solo, Mozart's haunting melody filled the room.

Molly rubbed her temple. "I don't understand," she whined. "You mean write a list of words?"

"Descriptions," Grayson clarified. "Write down anything the music brings to your mind."

"That's not easy," Dora said, her brow knitted.

"You really want me to write my thoughts down, Gray?" Bunnie giggled. Placing his forefinger against his lips, Grayson whispered, Shhhhhh. We must have silence so our creative juices can flow."

What am I doing with these crazies, Flora thought? She glared at her twin. All I do is humor that woman lately.

The music intensified as a violin and alto horn blended with the flute. Nancy and Bunnie began to scribble Molly's paper remained blank as she stared into space. Dora laboriously started writing, then paused, wondering how Nancy and Bunnie heard so much more from the sultry music.

Grayson stopped the tape. "Now who wants to be first?" He asked, standing at the podium.

"Censor mine, it's x-rated." Bunnie laughed.

"Mine sounds like a recipe for devil's food cake," Dora said. "I'm embarrassed to read it."

"I just put down a few errands and a grocery list," Nancy confessed. "I guess I'm not in the mood to be creative."

"Well," Grayson smirked. "I won't burden you with my effort. You'd probably all be jealous. Music inspires me, but I'll save this for some time in the future."

Molly stared at her blank paper. "I feel terrible. I couldn't think of anything."

"More refreshments, ladies." Grayson passed the sandwich tray. "I hope Bunnie and Flora will have their poems ready next week. Coffee for everyone?"

"Vodka on the rocks for me." Bunnie requested.

"Chardonnay is all I have, anyway you're driving."

"O.K., just black coffee, then. I'm no wino."

"Ladies, I have a wonderful idea for next week. "Let's use some facet of nature as a theme for our poem."

"Good," Flora mumbled under her breath, "I'll write my Garden of Death."

Molly peered at Grayson. "I guess Darla left for the studio already.

There wouldn't be a chance of bumping into her on the elevator, would there?" she asked, putting on her jacket.

"'Fraid not, it's quiet up there for a change." Noticing the disappointment in Molly's eyes, he added, "maybe if you come early next week, I'll introduce you."

- 6 -

At dusk Grayson's mouth gaped open as he glimpsed the naked woman plummet past his window. Jumping up from the couch, he ran on to the balcony.

Below, a small crowd gathered around the body.

Coatless and breathless, he emerged from the building joining them. Foghorns moaned intermingling with startled reactions.

"Wow! Did you see that?"

"Horrible, horrible, can't believe this!"

"That's Darla Rhodes, you know, the radio advice lady," a woman announced, leaning toward the body.

"Cover her," another woman in a maroon bathrobe, instructed. "Somebody put a coat over her. She looks indecent!

Two teenage boys gawked as a bearded man threw his coat over her.

Grayson edged nearer. He rubbed his eyes. She resembled a broken porcelain doll. Smashed pink-rimmed reading glasses lay a few feet away.

A teenage girl tried to grab them.

"Don't touch those," Grayson shouted. "Put them back where they were."

The girl obeyed, dropping the glasses. "I just wanted something to remember her by."

"Damn souvenir seekers," a white-haired man with a Yorkshire Terrier, muttered. He scooped up the dog into his arms.

"Why would she jump?" a lady in sweats asked.

"Those celebrities, who knows?" the white-haired man turned from the body. He placed the dog on the sidewalk. Ambling away from the scene, his lips formed the word, "nuts."

The lady in sweats, watching him, smirked, "She must have been crazy, not wearing a stitch."_

"Has someone called the police?" Grayson questioned the onlookers. The roar of a motorcycle answered him.

"Step back, clear the way," a booted officer instructed.

"She lived right above me," Grayson volunteered. "I saw her fall past my window."

The policeman removed his helmet, looking over his sunglasses at Grayson, he said. "You're not thinking of taking any trips, are you?"

Grayson shook his head, as the squad car's brakes screeched. He crinkled his nose smelling the burnt rubber.

"Stand back, everyone stand back," an officer shouted.

The motorcycle patrolman pointed at Grayson. "He knew her, lived below her." "Stay around here, sir, Detective Dusty Merkel will want to speak to you."

Grayson frowned asking, "Does he want to meet me here or do I have to go down to the station?"

"It's an official investigation, you'll have to go down to the station."

Grayson muttered under his breath, "I need another drink first."

- 7 -

"Damn," thought Grayson, what an ordeal. The cab stopped for a signal. Smart to leave my car at home. Scotch and driving is a dangerous mix. I'm too weary to drive, anyway.

Glimpsing the headlines on a corner newsstand, Grayson tapped on the glass divider. "You know, I was there today when Darla Rhodes jumped."

The cab driver, oblivious to Grayson's laments, crossed Market Street and turned up towards Telegraph Hill.

Grayson gave up and stared out of the back seat window at the banks of fog rising on the horizon. He pondered, was it an accident? Why would Darla jump willingly off her balcony?

The cab wound up the narrow hill, stopping in front of the white building on Darrel Place.

Grayson paid the driver without speaking. Before entering the foyer, he scanned the street. The body was gone from the pavement. Not even a chalk outline remained.

An ambulance must have deposited Darla at the morgue hours ago.

Grayson wiped his brow. Can't stand here gawking. He sped toward the elevator. Riding up, he recalled the last stressful hours.

You couldn't say Detective Dusty Merkel wasn't cordial. Quite different from the Dusty he remembered. The chubby-faced little boy had grown into a beefy partly-bald man. Pressing his temple, Grayson wondered would his head ever stop throbbing? How that man questioned me. I told him everything I knew. He could still hear his own voice, "In my opinion, it was a tragic accident."

Dusty rubbed the stubble on his chin. "That's a distinct possibility."

"I can't see why you're in doubt?"

"In my line of work," Dusty pulled a silver pen out of an ornate holder."

Grayson's eyebrows raised. That pen holder looked out of place.

Dusty read his mind. "A Father's Day present," He held the pen in front of Grayson, "Sterling Silver."

Grayson nodded.

"There is always doubt in a case like this. You may have forgot, but there's a four-foot guard rail surrounding that balcony. She didn't roller skate, did she?"

"What!" Grayson wasn't sure he heard the question.

"That would be one way she could topple over by accident. But, come to think of it, her feet were bare."

Grayson stared blankly at Dusty. Was he trying to be funny? He rubbed the back of his neck. Was there a draft from the open window? Maybe he could hurry this along. "All I know is I was sitting there when her body sailed past my living room window. We were only neighbors for two weeks."

He started to rise. "Is that it?"

"Sit back down," Dusty droned. "Now you didn't hear anything before it happened?"

"No, for a change there wasn't any noise, or maybe I got accustomed to the racket up there."

"You didn't hear any fighting or loud screams?"

Grayson leaned back. "I don't think it was suicide. There wasn't any note. Besides who would put on reading glasses to commit suicide?"

"You've got it figured out, huh, Grayson. Remember, in police investigations, we must never jump to hasty conclusions. All factors in a case must be considered." Dusty placed the pen back in the holder. "And that's my job."

Didn't think that questioning would ever end, Grayson leaned against the rear wall in the elevator. He scowled picturing Dusty's face. Traces of arrogance still remained after all these years. Forget boyhood memories and think logically.

Suicide did seem plausible. Why did he express his doubts to Dusty?

Maybe there wasn't a note because Darla didn't like to write. She might have been illiterate, for all I know. Booze is a depressant, I've heard. The way she hit the bottle every night, she probably was so drunk she thought she could fly off that balcony. Yet, what about those glasses? You'd think she'd wear something, too, even that blue teddy. And yet, she could have been an exhibitionist. Who else would jump off a building stark naked?

The guy who was staying with her, that Donald Palmcroft, has disappeared. Why does Dusty think I knew anything about him? I told him what I observed. He was some kind of jock who did push-ups at midnight between partying.

I hope the police find him and clear up this mess.

The elevator door slid open. Bewildered, Grayson found himself in front of the penthouse. The mahogony door was ajar, beckoning him to enter. Trance-like, he obeyed.

Every lamp was lit. Had the police been here? Of course, they must have investigated this place earlier. Sloppy of them to leave the door open and no yellow tape sealing the entrance.

The living room with its beamed ceiling didn't show any signs of partying. No empty glasses or dishes on the tables.

Grayson walked down the hall. The door to the master bedroom was wide-open. "Good God!" he blinked. You need sunglasses. Darla should have chosen more subtle shades. That bright pink and purple together is an interior decorator's nightmare._

Wading through rumpled piles of clothing, Grayson mumbled, "What a mess." Strange, with a wardrobe like this, she didn't have anything to wear in the end. Out of habit, he smoothed the polka-dot sheets. Looks almost as if she struggled with someone in bed. He draped the purple spread over the satin sheet. Something half-buried caught his eye. He yanked it out. "Oh my God!" he exclaimed. "This is a purple letter 'P' from one of our 'Power of Poetry' jackets." He stuck it into his pocket. Funny, the police overlooked it. Well, it probably wouldn't mean anything to them. Now, which one of the jackets is missing a "P." Scratching his head, he wondered, how well did he really know those ladies? He remembered how they sat around the large oval table at his poetry class every Monday afternoon along with twenty others. The University's budget prevented the poetry for adults class to continue. Those five were so disappointed. They talked him into supervising the poetry club. Yes, they were serious even if they lacked talent. Would one of my loyal ladies commit murder?

Tomorrow I'll phone them, invite them over, and do some detective work of my own.

- 8 -

"Such a tragedy," Molly said, wringing her hands.

Nancy patted Molly's shoulder. "I can't believe it."

They huddled on Nancy's beige couch, their eyes focused on the twenty-four inch screen.

"This is a special memorial tribute to Darla Rhodes, beloved radio personality died tragically last night."

The announcer's voice choked. "We will miss you, Darla. We love you."

"I'll miss you too, Darla," Molly sniffed. "Now I'll never get a chance to meet and thank you." She pulled a tissue from the box nestling between them. "So young, it isn't fair... I can't believe she's really dead."

Nancy watched her crumple the tissue and throw it on the carpet. "Here," she said, placing a small wicker basket in front of her.

"If you ask me, something seems fishy."

"What do you mean, Molly?"

"I don't know, but it's hard to believe a person like Darla just fell off that balcony."

"Considering the guard rail, it's unlikely," Nancy's brow knit. "Maybe the afternoon news will have more information.

The phone in the hall jingled..

"Good," the commercials on." Nancy rose from the couch, frowning as Molly tossed a waded tissue, missing the basket. Picking up the receiver on the fifth ring, she uttered a dismal, "hello."

Molly blew her nose as she watched a snowy-haired woman hold up a can of cat food. "'Kitty Delight' every feline's favorite. Two striped cats danced a jig around the can as the woman sang. "'Kitty Delight,' oh, 'Kitty Delight' is purrfectly wonderful food. Vitamins, minerals, and goodies all cats crave, plus discount coupons that you save."

Tears slid down Molly's cheeks.

Nancy slumped in, her face grim. "That was Grayson."

"I guess he knows about Darla."

"Let me turn this off," Nancy said, flicking the switch on the remote.

"Sure, he was home when it happened. That's what he wants to talk about."

"Why didn't he just tell you over the phone? I'm so upset, "He said it was important that we all meet with him. He sounded very evasive."

Molly's eyes widened, "What in the world?"

"Come on Molly, let's go."

"I don't know why I'm takin' it so hard. After all, we didn't really know her." Molly crumbled a tissue and aimed for the basket. It dropped two inches short.

"Goodness knows, it upsets me too," Nancy said, trying to overlook the crumpled bits on the carpet.

"Such a tragedy, I still can't believe it. She was an angel."

Nancy nodded. "A saint."

"Maybe she needed somebody to advise her?"

"Oh, I forgot, Grayson said we should wear our black poetry jackets. He's going to phone the others."

- 9-

Flora, armed with a paint brush, highlighted the letters on her sign. Satisfied, she leaned it against the garage wall. Walking a few feet away, she read the message: EQUAL RIGHTS FOR ALL ANIMALS.

Good, she thought, short and to the point. Didn't waste any words. Wait a minute, something's wrong. Dipping her brush in the black paint, she added at the bottom: EXCEPT RATS.

Maybe I should include snails, too. Even Marcia Welllkirk uses snail bait in her rose garden. Flora glanced at her watch. No, not enough time, I'm late for the meeting now.

Marching down Buena Vista Avenue, she held the sign high all the way to the brick house on the corner.

The seven members of the AMICABLE ANIMALS ASSOCIATION, seated around Marcia Wellkirk's dining room table, frowned as Flora entered.

"Where are we going to protest today? I hear there's a furrier downtown that's having a sale on leopard coats."

Groans echoed from the table.

Marcia's brow furrowed as all eyes turned toward her. "Why did I ever sponsor her?" she muttered under her breath.

"I just finished this," Flora waved her sign. "I'm rarin' for action." Marcia shuddered, thinking, I'd better say something. The others are holding me responsible. "All you want to do is march in front of some poor merchant's store. We're having a non-protest meeting this morning."

"How boring," Flora said, still holding her sign.

Dwight Fullerton put on his glasses. "What's that about rats on the bottom?"

"Just what it says. I don't like rats."

Dwight stood. "She's defeating our purpose, he shouted.

"The woman's nuts," another voice blared.

"She doesn't really care about animals," someone yelled. "Kick her out!"

Marcia pounded the small gavel. "Order, order, we must have order."

"Let me speak," Dwight asked, glaring at Flora. "Our group protects all creatures from cruelty. Remember, our motto, all creatures deserve equal rights."

Flora scowled. "Yes, but some animals are more equal than others. For instance, you wouldn't put a panda in the same category as a sewer rat, would you?"

"That's prejudice," a lady clad in a navy tailored suit screamed. "Yes, yes, right on," the others cheered.

"She really doesn't belong in the group," whispered Marcia, trying to calm the lady. "It's all my fault."

"She doesn't have any empathy for our cause," the woman responded.

"Order, order," Marcia announced.

Ignoring her, all the members began to shout.

"Can you imagine, some creatures more equal than others?"

Shielding herself with her sign, Flora tried to explain. "I'm for most animals, you people just don't understand. After all, I've supported this group. Damn it, I've marched with you at every protest."

Marcia banged the gavel.

"But what about those poor little white rats the labs use for all kinds of horrid experiments?" A lady at the end of the table asked. Flora's eyes darted from one angry face to another. Would they dare punch me, she wondered? Gripping her sign tighter, she smirked. "Rats is rats and..."

She was interrupted by banging on the front door.

There is a God, Marcia thought, seeing Dora on the doorstep.

"You've got to come with me at once," Dora said placing her plump hand on Flora's shoulder. "Grayson phoned and wants to see us. He said it's very important."

Flora, still waving her sign, followed Dora. She glared back at the group. "Well I guess I can't march today."

Cheers sounded.

- 10 -

"Pooh!" Flora grumbled. "There I was about to make my point when you rudely interrupted."

Dora slid into the Land Rover. "I'll drive."

Flora opened the passenger side door and sat next to her sister. Slumping in her seat, she pouted.

"You ought to be grateful I came. That mob had a look of 'lynch her' in their eyes." "They wouldn't dare. They respect my opinions."

"I'm sure. Oh, dear we have to go back home."

"Why?"

"To get your jacket, Grayson said it was vital we wear our jackets today."

"I don't want to wear that stupid jacket. Grayson, this Grayson that, who does he think he is 'The Great Dictator?"

"All right," Dora turned the Land Rover on to Fell Street. She slowed down, spotting a sign in front of Ralph's Market. "Look at that, they're having a sale on cat food. Do you think we have time to stop?"

"You told me Grayson wanted to see us right now," Flora snapped.

"Yes, that's true, but we're almost out of Kitty Delight."

"We can stop on the way back."

"Don't let me forget," Dora pressed the brake pedal as a traffic light changed to red.

"I won't."

Dora placed her foot back on the accelerator. "I finished a new poem last night."

"Already? You don't need it until next week." Why does she always try to show me up? Ever since grammar school, she acts as if we were in competition for some sort of prize. "O.K., sis, you win."

"Huh, win what?"

"Forget it," Flora sighed, telling herself to be nice. "What were you saying about your poem?"

Dora smiled. "I was a bit daring and experimented with Villanelle, it's my first in this form. I think Grayson will like it even if it is about cats."

Flora's mouth gaped in a yawn. "What the hell is Villanelle?"

"It's an intricate French verse form, with end-rhymes repeated and repeated key lines. I got this poetry book at the library," Dora explained.

"Sometimes," Flora reflected, thinking we're so different, "I wonder if I might have been adopted."

"That's ridiculous. We're identical twins."

Rolling her eyes in exasperation, Flora groaned. "You'll never understand."

Suddenly the Land Rover lurched. Dora glanced out the window, braking on the tracks in the center of the street. "Look over there, Flora!"

"Are you trying to kill us?" Flora cried, hearing a cable car's bell in back.

"Isn't that Donald coming out of that corner restaurant?"

"Sure looks like him."

Dora ignored the clanging. "Do you think I should wave or something?"

Twisting around, Flora glared at the cable car. She instructed her sister, "Get off these tracks before it runs into you."

"Oh dear," Dora moaned, edging the car off the tracks.

The cable car passed still clanging. Curling her fingers into an obscene gesture, Flora glared at the conductor.

Dora's face flushed. "Don't do that." She frowned, overlooking the stop sign on the corner.

"Told you, I should drive," Flora said with a smugness in her voice. "We're gonna' have an accident if you don't keep your mind on the road."

"Well, it upset me seeing Donald. Maybe I should have stopped?"

"What for?" You certainly don't want to start with him again."

"No," Dora said softly.

"There's Grayson's building, let's try to find a space."

"There's one," Dora pointed, "but I think it's too small. I'll never fit."

"Let me out, I'll direct you."

Flora slid out and stood on the sidewalk in front of the large white building.

Dora stopped the motor and stared at her sister. "To think you're standing in the place where Darla landed."

Flora shrugged. "I read somewhere somebody survived falling forty stories. Just got up and walked away, not a scratch on 'em."

"Don't want to hear about it," Dora yelled from the car's window. "It makes me too nervous."

"This way, Dora," Flora arm spun in a windmill like motion.

Dora pushed the gear in reverse, trying to follow Flora's instructions. She nodded as her sister's arm reversed, waving in the opposite direction.

The yellow hydrant remained steadfast accepting the impact of the Land Rover.

"Hold it!" Flora shouted. "You're backing into the hydrant."

"Why did you tell me to keep backing up?" Dora wailed.

"Oh no, I wasn't signaling you. Nancy and Molly just pulled up over there. I was waving at them."

"Is there much damage?"

Flora checked the rear of the Land Rover. "The hydrants O.K., but there's a dent on the back fender. You're still miles from the curb, do you want me to direct you?"

"I don't need your help." Dora maneuvered the Land Rover into the space.

- 11 -

"Good God! Gray, you look terrible!" Bunny exclaimed, her lips stretching into a half-smile. "Been partying too much?" "Yeah, the police and I were partying half the night at the station. We played 2,020 questions." "Why would they question you?" "I don't know?" Grayson clasped his forehead. "Maybe they think I had something to do with it since I saw her fall and live right below her." Bunny seated herself on the couch. "That's crazy, after all it was an accident, wasn't it?" "To tell you the truth, I don't really know?" Grayson's hand now cupped his chin. "She could have committed suicide or, perhaps even been pushed."

"Well, personally, I think she probably slipped and fell. It was an accident."

"With a four foot guard rail?"

"She drank a lot. I'll bet she was snockered."

"Tell Dusty Merkel, he's in charge." Grayson snickered.

"Dusty Merkel," Bunny repeated. "He's the same detective who's investigating Charlie's case." She grinned. "He can't figure out that one either." Her eyes searched the room. "Any coffee, Gray?" "I'll get you cup." He retreated into the kitchen.

Bunny followed. "Say Gray, why did you want us here? Are you gonna' spring some poetry quiz on us, or somethin'?"

He leaned against the counter, hands shaking, he poured coffee into two china cups. "I phoned everyone to meet here because I found something last night."

"What?" Bunny's penciled eyebrows raised an inch.

"I prefer to wait until everyone's here."

Sipping her coffee, Bunny teased. "Oh, come on Gray, you can tell me."

Grayson opened his mouth to speak, but the doorbell's chime interrupted.

"Damn, what timing," Bunny uttered, eyeing Molly and Nancy.

"You look terrible, Grayson," they chorused.

"Leave the door open," Nancy instructed, the Stromboli twins are right behind us."

Flora's voice snapping at her sister could be heard from the hallway. "It wasn't my fault."

Entering, she glared at Grayson. "O.K. what's so important? You disrupted my Amicable Animal Association meeting."

Dora looked up at Grayson, apologetically. "We can't stay too long. Ralph's Market is having a special on cat food today. We've got to get there before he closes at five."

"We have to buy "Kitty Delight" by the case now," Flora added.

Dora giggled. "Charlotte and Emily eat like they're part pig."

Grayson's eyes rolled toward the ceiling. "Please, no cat stories."

Ignoring him, Dora went on. "And poor little Lord Byron is slightly anorexic. I have to coax him even hand feed him."

"You spoil him," Flora interjected.

Removing a white handkerchief from his pocket, Grayson wondered, why does that woman insist upon cats as her main topic of conversation? He blew his nose. Even hearing about those creatures caused his allergies to react. He sneezed.

"God bless you," Molly acknowledged.

"Thank you," he said, inspecting Flora's white sweat shirt: "Return Rights To Animals," printed in blazing maroon letters across the back.

"Where's your 'Power of Poetry' jacket?"

Bobbing her head, Dora frowned. "See I told you, Flora. Grayson wanted us to wear our jackets. She scanned the room. Look, everyone else has their's on."

Pointing her index finger at her sister, Flora shouted. "What has that got to do with anything? You don't tell me what to wear."

Throwing her palms up, Dora sighed. "She doesn't listen to me at all."

Grayson voice was grim. "Flora, I wish you had worn the jacket. You see, I think there was foul play connected with Darla's death."

"What do you mean?" Molly asked. "The TV news said she fell. Nancy and I both heard it."

Bunny's eyes widened. "Gray, you mean you don't think it was an accident?"

"Do you know something we don't?" Nancy asked. "Ye...ye...yes, he stammered, "I'm afraid I do. Well, I might as well tell you. Last night, Dusty Merkel persisted in putting me through the third degree."

Molly made clucking sounds with her tongue. "That wasn't very nice."

"It wasn't very nice at all. With all his questioning, I was so exhausted when he released me, I must have pressed the wrong button on the elevator. Inadvertently, I ended up at Darla's penthouse. The door was open. Don't ask me why, but I went into her bedroom." He placed the felt purple "P" in the center of the coffee table.

"I found this in her bed."

"What was that doing there?" Molly reached for the "P." Holding it between her thumb and forefinger, she murmured. "It sure looks like one of our 'P's." Bunny gazed at the felt letter. "You think one of us was up there?"

Slumping on the couch, Grayson shook his head. "I don't know what to think."

"My God!" Dropping the 'P' on the table, Molly placed her hand over her heart. "You think one of us pushed her? All of us loved Darla. We would never do anything like that."

"I don't know," Grayson repeated, "I'm not sure what happened."

"How can you jump to such rash conclusions?" Nancy stared at Grayson.

"Come on, none of us are murderers, anyhow we all have our 'P's' intact."

"Except me." Flora's eyes blazed. "Is that it? I'm the only one who doesn't have a jacket on. Are you accusing me, Grayson?"

"Remember, Grayson said, "I didn't tell the police about this. He sighed. "I wanted to speak to you ladies, first."

"You didn't tell the police," Flora blared, "because you don't have anything to go on. They would wonder what you were doing in Darla's bedroom. Probably think you planted that 'P' in there."

Patting her sister's shoulder, Dora turned to face Grayson. "You surprise me."

"Yeah," Molly's eyes focused on the coffee table. "I'm disappointed in you suspecting one of us."

"Wait a minute, I'm not accusing anyone."

"Yes you are." Flora leered at Grayson. "You are accusing me just because I'm not wearing that damned jacket."

"Let's be calm," Nancy suggested. "Why would any of us want to kill Darla? There's no motive. We must look at this objectively before we start pointing fingers."

"Go ahead, call the police," Flora snapped.

"Don't get upset, dear." Dora hugged her sister. "We'll just go home and get your jacket."

"That will show you, Mister Accuser," Molly put her arm on Flora's shoulder.

"I need a cigarette," Bunny slid the glass door open and stepped out on the balcony. Her face a vivid crimson, Flora sneered. "You just wait, we'll show you that jacket."

"After you sew another 'P' on it?" Grayson muttered.

Tilting her head, Molly pondered. "You know, she could. It wouldn't be that hard."

Flora brushed Molly's hand off her shoulder. "Who's side are you on?" Grayson pointed to the coffee table. "That is definitely from one of the jackets."

"Where's your jacket, Grayson," Nancy asked.

"Here, I'll show you." Pulling the garment from the hall closet, he held it up. "Power of Poetry," was written in flawless purple letters.

"I don't know?" Molly's face paled. "All this is making my stomach kind of queasy."

"Maybe I should stick to my pottery class." Nancy said, putting on her own jacket.

"Ceramantists murder as well as poets," Molly whined. "Come on Nancy." Leaning toward the Strombolis, she instructed. "You just show Grayson Flora's jacket. That'll put an end to all of this."

"Come on Molly, let's leave."

"We're going to leave, too," Dora said, starting for the door.

Without saying goodbye, Grayson looked out on the balcony at Bunny. Good, she put the cigarette out.

"Now that the others have left, may I talk to you?" he asked, sliding the door open.

"What do you want to know?"

"Dusty Merkel wonders where your friend, Donald Palmcroft is? You don't have any ideas, do you?"

Bunny shook her head. Staring at Grayson, she pulled a cigarette from the pack and waved it threateningly at him.

"Don't," he advised. "Were you ever married to him?"

"Heavens no, he was just a passing fancy between my first and second," Bunny hesitated, "or was it between my third and fourth?"

"You should keep better track."

"Don't mock me. How can I make it plainer. I don't see that creep anymore."

Looking back through the glass, Grayson gasped. Flora stood by the coffee table listening.

- 12 -

Poor Flora, Molly thought, hanging her poetry jacket in the hall closet. How could Grayson think she had something to do with Darla's death.

There was a sharp rap at the front door.

"Coming, coming," Molly announced.

Her mouth gaped open. Standing on the welcome mat was a thin, brown-haired girl.

"Pepper Finkel," Molly gasped.

"I've decided to leave Leon and come home," Pepper said, dragging a denim duffel bag into the living room.

"But dear," Molly's eyes grew larger. "This is not your home."

"Well," Pepper explained. "Since my folks are both remarried and living in Europe, this is the closest place to home I got."

Suddenly dizzy, Molly grasped the table for support. "But this is Leon's home, you're my daughter-in-law." She glared at Pepper suspiciously. "Where's Leon?"

Tears formed in Pepper's eyes. "Back in Chicago. We had a stupid argument," she sniffed.

Patting the girl's shoulder, Molly handed her a tissue.

"Tell me what happened?"

Pepper inhaled.

"Wait, before you begin," Molly asked. "Where are my grandsons?

"Oh, they're fine, Mom, we sent them to camp."

Molly cringed. She never called me Mom before. She's certainly confused. Oh, what's the difference. I'll wait until she calms down.

"Your son resents me having a career," Pepper began.

"You mean he doesn't want you working in that coffee shop anymore? That's good, isn't it?"

"No, I mean my new career." Glancing at her watch, Pepper stopped crying. "In about five minutes you'll see me on TV." Staring at her with new respect, Molly wondered why she hadn't noticed talent in her daughter-in-law before. "You're an actress now?"

Pepper grinned.

"What happened to your teeth?" Molly gasped.

Pepper kept grinning.

She's almost pretty now, Molly reflected, but she's acting cuckoo.

"I finally had them bonded and capped with no financial help from your son." Pulling a small mirror from her bag, Pepper smiled at her reflection. "Leon said I looked fine the way I was. Too cheap to give me the money. I'm paying for these myself." She pointed to her front teeth, "from my royalties."

"Royalties?" Molly repeated, studying the duffel bag. "Is that all you brought?"

Ignoring her, Pepper commanded, "Turn on the TV."

An assortment of feet filled the screen as a baritone voice announced, "Do you have painful corns on your toes?" The camera zoomed in for a close up on a foot with a red induration on the small toe.

Tearing off her sock, Pepper stuck her left foot out. "That's my foot, see I still have the corn on my little toe."

Molly's eyes shifted from the screen to Pepper's foot. "Yes, that's your toe all right."

A jingle started. Pepper wiggled her toes to the tempo. "Painful corns will soon disappear. You'll walk with ease using Dermisqueeze."

"You use that?" Molly asked.

"Not yet, even though they sent me a free tube. I want people to recognize my foot."

"Doesn't that corn hurt?"

"Oh, a little. You know everytime that commercial is aired, they send me a check."

Molly scratched her head. "How much has your foot made?"

"Actually, nothing yet, but the checks will start coming soon." Kicking the duffel bag, she confided, "I plan to buy a new wardrobe."

Molly studied her daughter-in-law with disbelief. "They pay for your corn?"

"Sure, the Finkel foot is famous."

"And Leon doesn't like this?"

"Your son," Pepper pouted,"doesn't want me to be on TV. He says that's not the Finkel foot." "It looks the same."

"Leon's just stubborn. He'll change when he sees my royalty checks."

"So," Molly wondered if it was appropriate to ask? "You plan on staying here?"

Pepper nodded. "In Leon's old room, if that's all right?"

She didn't wait for Molly to answer. "Tomorrow, I will make the rounds. There are other parts of me," she displayed her teeth. "that television can use."

- 13 -

Marching up the walkway toward the Victorian, Bunny wondered. Why did Flora Stromboli invite me over?

Heartly strained on his leash sniffing at the border of marigolds. He stared at a robin hopping on the lawn. "Come on Heartly, remember you're a hound, not a bird dog."

She dragged him in front of the thick oak door.

"Come in, the door's open," Flora's voice from inside instructed.

Bunny twisted the brass knob. The door creaked open. Pulling Heartly inside the wood paneled foyer, Bunny cringed glancing at the sparse furnishings in the living room. This place is a dump, she thought gazing at the faded green curtains and worn-out rug.

Just as I expected, neither one of those Stromboli's has any taste. She sniffed. This place reeks of cats.

"Don't you lock your door?" Bunny asked, seeing Flora at the top of the stairs.

"It's one of those double-bolted locks, Dora always has trouble locking it." The steps squeaked as Flora edged down. Frowning at the dog, she said, "I hope he likes cats."

"Heartly doesn't even know what a cat is."

"Come into the living room."

Picking up Heartly, Bunny followed Flora into the large room. "You can sit there." Flora pointed to a faded settee with a frayed petti-point cushion.

Bunny's eyes swept around the room. This place gives me the creeps. "Where's Dora?"

"At the beauty salon."

Bunny raised her eyebrows. "I thought she did her own hair," refraining from blurting, the way it looks, I didn't think it was a professional job.

"She usually does. But she wanted to get gussied up special for her date."

"Dora's dating?" Bunny grinned.

"That's why I asked you over. I hear you know Donald Palmcroft?"

"Aren't the police looking for him?" Bunny clutched Heartly tighter.

"I don't know. He started phoning Dora again. Says he's disturbed about a deep dark secret."

"Secret," Bunny repeated.

"Yeah, I think it's crazy too. That man's a womanizer. I wish Dora would realize he's only interested in her money."

A large orange cat slinked in.

Heartly growled, then let out a sharp yip."

"Keep your mutt quiet, he's frightening poor Charlotte."

Bunny glared at the cat, now rubbing against Flora's garden boots.

"Heartly's no mutt. He's a registered pedigreed Italian Greyhound."

"Doesn't matter to me, a dog's a dog." Tell me about this Donald?" Flora asked again.

"Nothing to tell," Bunny shrugged, gazing at the dining room table in the adjoining room.

A plate of glazed doughnuts graced the table. You'd think she offer me one or at least a cup of coffee.

Rising to her feet, Bunny shrugged. "This is a complete waste of my time."

"Are you leaving?" Flora asked, stroking the cat's fur.

"I have another appointment," Bunny lied.

"Well," Flora said, still seated, "I thought you knew something about this Donald."

- 14 -

Exhausted, Grayson turned over on his left side in the king-sized bed. "Clear your mind, get some sleep," he repeated. Maybe it was too quiet in here without the noise from the late parties at the penthouse. Why couldn'tsleep? Closing his eyes, he tried to blank out all thoughts.

The white painted lines on the cruel cement yard of Alexander Hamilton Elementary School loomed in his mind. He groaned, hearing, "Sissy, sissy boy." Dusty's voice was louder than the others.

Why should memories of incidents in the second-grade playground emerge now? Go back to sleep, he told himself. Seeing Dusty again after all these years, that's what did it. Brought back all those forgotten nightmares of the past.

He turned over on his right side, but still forty-year old memories interrupted.

Ironic, Dusty chose a career on the police force. He visualized Dusty on the other side of the law. Dusty, that sadistic little bastard, would haunt him forever.

He remembered the brick house with the large back yard.

"Let's play cowboys and Indians. Joey and I will be the cowboys, and you, Grayson can be the Indian."

"Dusty, why can't Joey be an Indian, too?"

"Cause there's gotta be more cowboys to hunt the Indian."

"Well then, why can't I be a cowboy sometimes?"

"Cause you're the Indian, Grayson. A very bad Indian. We gotta catch you and bring you to justice."

Grayson was easy prey, not hard to find huddled in back of the shed. His chest twitched, still feeling the taut rope as they tied him to the oak's trunk.

"Take off his pants, and his underpants, too," Dusty instructed Joey.

Dusty sneered, not satisfied, seeing Grayson squirm naked against the rough bark. "Let's burn him at the stake. That's what they do to bad Indians. Come on, Joey, help me."

Gathering sticks, the boys placed them around the roots of the tree. Grayson screamed, pulling at the rope. Dusty's talent in tying knots, made it impossible to wiggle out. Dusty and Joey, deaf to his sobs, continued adding wood and paper to the pyre.

Mrs. Merkel, washing dishes, looked out of the window above the sink to see her son light a match.

"Heck," Dusty grumbled, "this wood is moist. It won't burn. We need more matches."

"Are you boys crazy?" Mrs. Merkel yelled, rushing into the yard. She untied Grayson who tore up the street naked, yelping like a wounded pup.

"We were just playin'," Dusty said, innocently as she snatched the book of matches from his hand.

Dusty's eyes were red and swollen at school the next day. He must have received one hell of a whipping. Still his jeers didn't stop when he spotted Grayson hiding behind the monkey bars. "Sissy, sissy, Grayson is a sissy boy."

"Shut up!" Grayson shouted, sitting up in bed. He wiped his forehead. Gad, he was perspiring. How could an incident in his childhood upset him so now?

After he confided to his father, he enrolled in a private school. He seldom saw Dusty after that.

Dropping his head on the pillow, he drew the blanket close to his chin. He focused on the events of the past few days. If only Darla hadn't decided to move above him. In only a couple of weeks, she managed to disrupt his whole life.

"Oh," he groaned, why did he have to find that damn "P?" What was he thinking of exploring Darla's bedroom? Great, now he suspected one of his ladies of murder. How could he presume one of them had anything to do with Darla's death?

He pictured Flora's angular face. Maybe she had a crusty exterior, definitely no poetic ability, but was she capable of murder?

"What about that exercise freak, Donald Palmcroft? Where had he disappeared to? Too many unanswered questions, leave the detective work to Dusty.

He closed his eyes, telling himself, stop thinking, make your mind a blank.

Suddenly, the phone on the night stand rang, jarring him into startling consciousness. He reached for the ivory-colored receiver.

"Hello," he mumbled.

"Grayson," the frightened voice asked.

"Flora, is that you?" What the hell would she want disturbing me at this time of night?"

"Oh Grayson, I didn't want to call the police. I hope you can help me."

Was the woman weeping, he wondered?

"I don't know what to do?"

"Calm down, Flora, tell me what's wrong?"

"I know, Grayson. I know who's responsible for Darla's death. It wasn't an accident or suicide, I know who murdered her."

"What do you know?" Grayson sat upright. "Tell me, who did it?"

Her voice faded. She wasn't speaking to him any longer. "What are you doing here? Honestly I didn't think it was you. Oh, my God, stay away from me!"

"No don't!" he yelled into the receiver. "Who's there?"

He gasped, hearing an ear-shattering scream. He dropped the phone.

Retrieving it, he shouted, "Hello, hello, Flora, what's going on? Flora, answer me." The dial tone sounded at the other end.

He banged the receiver down for a minute. Picking it up again, he quickly pressed the buttons.

There was no answer after seven rings. He tried again.

There's no other choice, he thought.

"Police Department," a voice answered.

"Is Detective Merkel there?"

"Just a moment, I'll connect you."

"No, no don't connect me. It doesn't matter. Send someone to 23 Buena Vista Terrace, the Victorian on the corner. Oh, yes I'm Grayson Crown, Detective Merkel knows me. Please hurry, I thin something horrible happened." Grayson repeated, "hurry!"

With a trembling hand he replaced the receiver.

He tried the Stromboli number. Still no answer.

He ran to the closet, grabbed an overcoat to conceal his pale blue silk pajamas and tore out of the condo.

In the garage, he turned the ignition, starting the silver compact.

Turning into the Victorian's wide driveway. he spotted two police cars, their lights flashing like fires against the foggy sky.

"Where do you think you're going?" One of the officers placed his hand on Grayson's shoulder.

"I'm Grayson Crown, I phoned you earlier. What happened?"

"How well acquainted are you with the Stromboli's?"

"They're in my poetry group," Grayson looked toward the house. Lights shone from every window. "Tell me, what's going on? Are the women all right?"

The officer shook his head. "We've got a dead body in there."

"Oh my God!"

"Maybe you can help us identify her?"

The color drained from Grayson's face. "Do I have a choice?"

He followed the policemen into the house.

"She's in the hall, upstairs."

Knees quivering, Grayson walked up the steep wooden steps. His stomach churned seeing a lump covered by a dark blanket at the top.

Pulling the blanket away, the officer asked, "Do you know her?"

Grayson's throat constricted as he looked at the distorted features. He coughed, holding back an urge to retch.

Splatters of blood surrounded the body. God, how many times had her flesh been ripped? "I know her," he gagged. It's Flora Stromboli. "Do you know of anyone that would want her dead?"

The officer replaced the blanket.

Grayson exhaled. Wiping his brow, he shook his head.

The policeman started jotting in a notebook. "Your name?" he asked. Grayson face turned ashen. On the policeman's thumb was a drop of crimson blood.

"Your thumb," he said.

"Yeah, the officer rubbed his hands against his sleeve. "Ready for the cleaners anyway. These cases get kinda messy."

Uncouth, Grayson thought, averting is eyes from the officer. "Is Dora all right?"

Ignoring his question, the policeman instructed, "Follow us down to the station. Detective Merkel will want to ask you some questions."

Another trip to Bryant Street. Grayson groaned, wondering, could he tolerate facing Dusty again. "Do I have a choice?"

The officer grinned, "No way."

Starting his car engine, Grayson wondered, where was Dora?

The officer in the white police car waved to him. Grayson followed.

- 15 -

"Right in here," the uniformed officer said.

"I know," Grayson answered, entering the familiar office.

Dusty Merkel spun his chair around facing Grayson. "Here we go again, eh, Grayson." He scratched his thinning hair. "How come you're always around when there's an unexplained body?" Dusty smirked. "You know that don't look too good."

Grayson sat erect in a straight-backed chair. Probably use these uncomfortable chairs on purpose.

Dusty's desk faced him. Odd, he hadn't noticed the photograph before. His eyes lingered on the large blonde woman in the foreground displaying a pronounced overbite. A small boy stood by her side, grinning. Grayson's body stiffened. That child was an impish clone of Dusty at that age.

"My family," Dusty leaned back in his chair. "Selma and little Dusty, a chip off the old block. You never married, eh, Grayson?"

Grayson was silent.

Dusty didn't notice. His eyes scanned a report on the desk. Looking at Grayson, he said, "Tell me what you know about this Stromboli stabbing."

Grayson shifted his position. Looking Dusty straight in the eye, he admitted. "I was talking to Flora Stromboli on the phone when it happened."

"Did she say anything about the intruder?"

"No," Grayson lied. "As a matter of fact, we were discussing a poem she wrote. She wanted advice on a technical matter. She left the phone for a minute to get another sheet of paper, and never returned." Grayson's eyes strayed back to the photo. Uncanny how that kid resembled Dusty.

"Still into poetry, Grayson? Heard you taught at the college for a while?"

"Financial problems, they ran out of money for my program. Now I head a small poetry group." Staring down at his slippered bare feet, Grayson wished he had the foresight to put on socks. It was chilly in here.

"What's that saying, all the world loves a poet," Dusty snickered.

"I think you got that wrong."

"Well, whatever," Dusty's thick fingers picked up the silver pen. "Go on with your story."

"There isn't much more," Grayson cleared his throat. "I heard Flora scream. That's when I phoned you. Then I decided to drive over there myself. You know the rest."

"The way we figure," Dusty scribbled on the pad. "Someone thought both sisters were out of the house, broke in and must have panicked when they saw Flora on the phone."

Grayson squirmed. Should he ask for a pillow? No, he reconsidered, bad idea. Still gazing at the photo, he asked, "Where was her sister, Dora? They're usually together."

"She wasn't home as far as we know."

"You think it was a burglar, then?"

"That's a strong possibility, but most burglars would have fled seeing her. Burglars usually rob, not kill people."

"It was ghastly what he did to that poor woman," Grayson shuddered, remembering the grotesque expression on Flora's face.

"Multiple stab wounds in a burglary doesn't set right with me."

"All that blood." Grayson eyes returned to the photo, analyzing the boy's familiar menacing grin. Grimacing at the image, he thought, what a strong argument for abortion.

Dusty didn't notice and went on in an emotionless voice. "Murder is never pretty."

"Who would want Flora Stromboli dead? What reason could there possibly be?"

"Afraid playing detective is my job, Grayson, unless you know something you're not telling me." "No," Grayson stammered, avoiding looking directly at him. "Just don't understand why someone would stab Flora?"

Scrawling a few marks on the pad, Dusty smiled. "That's what we'll find out."

Grayson wrapped the coat tighter. How ridiculous to sit here in blue silk pajamas. Should I tell Dusty the truth? Who am I trying to protect anyway? It's Dusty's attitude. He hasn't changed at all since we were in grade school. Still, he rationalized, why am I deliberately trying to mislead him.

Placing the pen back in its holder, Dusty read from his paper. "According to my records, when old Angelo died, he left his daughters pretty well off. It's no secret about the large amount of cash kept in that house."

"Yes, Flora had an aversion to banks. She harbored some strange notion the bank manager was going to abscond with her savings. Dora confided to me once, she couldn't get her sister to even open a checking account."

"Go on," Dusty said.

"Dora told me she hated having all that cash around. They argued about it often. I guess she was right."

Dusty resumed writing. "You said the sisters argued? Did they fight often?"

"You misunderstood me. They were inseparable, twins you know."

"Identical?" Dusty asked.

"I've heard you couldn't tell them apart when they were children. Of course, they look entirely different now."

"I see."

Grayson tried to read what Dusty was writing. Even right side up Dusty's handwriting was impossible. "Was anything taken from the house?" he asked.

Dusty shook his head, still writing. "Nothing appeared touched. When Dora returns, we can take inventory. My theory is the intruder wasn't a professional, probably a junkie looking for easy money. Possibly he was even high, could have been hallucinating. I hear Flora had quite a temper.

She could have panicked and gone at him."

Yes, Grayson thought, remembering the last poetry session. Flora did have a temper.

"She must have frightened him so that he slashed her. Then seeing what he did, he got the hell out of there without taking a penny. Yeah, that's the way I see it."

Inserting his hands in the coat's pockets, Grayson shivered. "Isn't rather chilly in here?"

"The heater's on the blink. Anything else you want to tell me? May I suggest you go directly home and get some sleep, you don't look too good, Grayson."

"Yes, that's exactly what I plan to do." Now he acts as If I volunteered to come down here. He started to rise. "Am I free to leave now?"

"Oh, sure. I appreciate your help. Cases like this form a pattern, they're not that unusual. I've solved maybe a hundred or more like this during my career." Pointing to a plaque framed in black plastic, he continued. "The department presented that to me last year."

"Congratulations," Grayson said without even glancing at the award.

"Yeah, we'll find the bastard that did this."

- 16 -

"Can you believe it, the coroner won't release Flora's body so I can give her a decent burial," Dora sobbed.

Molly clucked in sympathy, rubbing her finger on the maple end table. Not a trace of dust. That Nancy is some housekeeper.

"Did they tell you when you can have poor Flora?" Nancy asked. "They won't tell me anything. My own dear sister is lying on some slab and I can't claim her." Dora extended her cup, allowing Nancy to refill it with hot coffee.

"Bureaucracy, that's what it is," Nancy set the coffee pot on the table. "There's so much red tape involved. Pretty soon you'll need official approval to walk across the street."

"By the grace of God," Dora's hands trembled as she raised the cup to her lips. "Do you realize it could have been me."

"Let's talk about something else," Nancy suggested. "How's your daughter-in-law, Molly?"

"Depressed," Molly added two lumps of sugar to her coffee. The teaspoon clinked as she stirred. "She's had no luck finding another TV job. Leon phoned last night, and I think she's ready to go back to him."

"That's wonderful, she's come to her senses." Nancy said,.

Molly didn't answer. Yes, Pepper was a little crazy, but she had the same rebellious streak that I had at her age. Did Leon inherit Seymour's nature? But, that would be impossible.

Dora droned, "We came home from the poetry session at Grayson's."

"Oh, Dora, Nancy said, not mentioning that she knew the story by heart already. "You don't want to go over it again."

"No, that's all right," Dora swallowed a sip of coffee and continued.

"Flora and I were working on our poems. I always like to get mine written early."

"Me too," Molly chirped.

"Poor Flora," Dora choked, "was so eager to write about nature."

"That's a surprise," Nancy commented. "I didn't think she cared about poetry."

"Yes," Dora blew her nose, "Usually she wasn't very enthused. Well to get back to my story. I was busy with my new poem. You know how time flies when you're creating? Charlotte and Emily came in and starting meowing. It dawned on me, the little dears were hungry."

"Would you like another blue berry tart?" Nancy asked, "Just a small one, I haven't been able to eat since...well you know."

"They're all the same size," Nancy said, plopping one on Dora's plate.

"Go on Dora," Molly leaned forward.

"Flora usually attended to the cats, something to do with her animal rights activities. But, with Flora engrossed writing about a snail, I decided to feed them"

"That's hard to believe," Molly commented, winking at Nancy.

"I went to the cupboard and noticed there was only one can left. The way Charlotte and Emily eat, that wouldn't be enough. We feed them twice a day. Charlotte and Emily eat a whole can. Now Little Lord Byron turns up his nose at food. Sometimes, I think he lives on air." Dora took a large bite of the tart.

"That tastes homemade, Nancy. It's delicious."

Before giving Nancy a chance to answer, Dora went on. "I remember asking Flora if she wanted to drive with me to the All-Night Market. No, she said, I'd rather finish my poem."

Ignoring Nancy and Molly's confused looks, she went on.

"I went to the market, bought the Kitty Delight, and on the way back my tire went flat. I spent hours at that gas station, had to buy a new tire, you know." Dora dabbed a tear forming in her eye. "Why didn't I insist Flora come with me?"

"But you didn't know," Molly said, grasping Dora's hand.

"When I drove home, I saw all the lights and the police cars in front. They had removed Flora's body already. That's when I learned." She brushed crumbs off her ample lap, spilling them on the carpet.

Noticing the annoyed look on Nancy's face, she murmured, "Sorry, I'll pick them up. It's just I've been so upset since..."

"Don't bother, I was going to vacuum later."

Dora's eyes focused on the three tarts remaining on the platter.

"Maybe I could have another one?"

Tilting the platter, Nancy slid the remaining tarts on Dora's plate.

"You know." Dora spoke between mouthfuls, I haven't had much of an appetite since..."

"Poor dear," Molly comforted. "If those policemen would patrol the neighborhoods more often, they'd catch those burglars."

"You're right," Nancy answered, patting Dora's shoulder. "It isn't safe for anyone nowadays, even in your home."

"You know what was funny?" Dora swallowed. "I couldn't find anything missing in the whole house."

"Odd?" Nancy and Molly said together.

"That got me to thinkin' when the police asked me if Flora had any enemies. Flora didn't get along with most people."

"Now I got along with her," Molly volunteered.

"Oh, I'm not talking about you. But I'll have to admit Flora could get really nasty at times. In fact lots of people told her, right to her face, they would like to kill her."

"You mean there were threats against her life?" Molly's eyes opened wide.

"Dozens," Dora plopped the last tart in her mouth. She chewed and swallowed before continuing. "I told Detective Merkel all about them. Let's see there's the grocery clerk at Ralph's, the electrician who fixed our wiring last year, the refrigerator repair man, the television cable man, and the newspaper boy. Flora screamed at him because he threw the paper on her peonies. She claimed it was deliberate. You could hear them yelling at each other halfway down the block."

"That's terrible," Molly shook her head. "Does Detective Merkel suspect any of them?"

"I don't know, he may have to question almost everybody in San Francisco. An awful lot of people didn't like my sister. I forgot to mention the animal rights association looked at her with daggers in their eyes. I saved her life from that group only a few days ago."

"Oh dear," Molly moaned.

"Now I have to go back to that house alone," Dora wailed. I'm frightened."

"If it wasn't for those cats, you could stay here," Nancy gazed around the room. "I just had the sofa and chairs recovered, and even well-behaved cats may use them for a scratching post."

"I couldn't bear to be without Charlotte, Emily and Longfellow," Dora sobbed. They're the only family I have now."

"Dora," Molly suggested, her eyes twinkling. "Why not stay with me. My furniture is old, your cats couldn't damage it anymore than Seymour."

She gave Dora a playful pat. "They don't drink beer, or smoke cigars, do they?"

Dora shook her head. "But what about Pepper? Would you have room for all of us?", "Sure, I have an extra bedroom. Don't say another word, you're staying with me."

"And," Nancy added, "you're always welcome here minus felines."

Dora smiled. "I'll drive back home now and get some clothes and of course, my family."

"We'll go with you."

- 17 -

"What a beautiful day," Molly said, gazing out of the Land Rover's window at the clear blue sky.

Nancy squeezed closer to Molly, so Dora could shift as she turned left into Golden Gate Park.

Driving past a grove of Eucalyptus, Molly inhaled. "It sure smells good just like we were out in the country."

"There's less traffic if we cut through the park," Dora explained, wiping her nose with a tissue. "Poor Flora always enjoyed driving through here."

"Isn't that Spreckels Lake?" Nancy asked. "Slow down a little, Dora."

A group of children stood on the shore engrossed in watching a fleet of toy boats navigate. A flag signaled the beginning of a race. Cheers exploded as a tiny blue boat took the lead.

"Too noisy here," Dora applied more pressure to the accelerator.

"Look at that little lake ahead with all those cute ducks." Molly said smiling. "Can we stop a minute?"

Parking the Land Rover by some pine trees, Dora said, "Go ahead, take a stroll. We aren't in a big hurry."

"Aren't you coming?" Molly asked, stepping out on the path.

"You and Nancy go, I'll be there in a minute."

Loud quacks from the swimming birds lured Molly to the grassy shore.

"We should of brought some bread crumbs. When Leon was little, I used to take him to feed the ducks on Sundays."

Nancy gazed out at the clear water. How good it felt stretching her legs. It was too cramped with three in the front seat. Why did she insist on coming?

Molly interrupted. "A penny for your thoughts."

"Nothing important, not even worth a penny." Turning toward the Lane Rover, Nancy asked, "Where's Dora? Isn't she gonna' sit in there?"

Molly squinted in the bright sun. "No, she's getting out. What's she taking out of the back?"

"It's a plastic bag," Nancy responded.

"Where do you think she's gonna' do with that?"

"Let's just watch and see what she does."

Gripping the bag, Dora peered to the left and right.

"She doesn't see us," Molly whispered.

Satisfied, she crept down an overgrown trail, ending on the lake's far shore. "Darn, she's hidden from view," Nancy muttered. Before Molly could answer, they heard a splash.

A few minutes later, Dora appeared on the road across from them, waving.

"Did someone fall into the lake?" Nancy shouted.

"Heavens no," Dora yelled back.

"Where is that plastic bag you were carrying?" Molly asked as Dora walked toward them.

Dora's face flushed. "Oh that, it was just some extra garbage I wanted to get rid of."

Nancy gave her a righteous stare. "Isn't that illegal?"

Dora hung her head, explaining. "Yeah, but I had extra garbage that wouldn't fit in my can this week. You know bags of cat litter takes a lot of room."

Molly patted Dora's shoulder. "That's O.K., Dora. Nancy you don't want her to jump in the lake and retrieve it?"

"Just forgot it." Nancy studied the two women, wondering. This poetry group is really crazy. Maybe I should devote all my energy toward ceramics. In time I could learn to make a respectable looking jug.

Dora started for the Land Rover. "Come on Ladies, let's go."

- 18 -

The greenness was replaced by rows of pastel-colored houses as Dora swung the Land Rover out of the park. Shifting to second gear, she climbed the hill to Buena Vista Avenue. As they neared the top, the old Victorian loomed into view.

Nancy and Molly waited as Dora twisted the key in the front door. "I always have problems with this lock," she apologized.

The heavy oak door finally clicked open.

"This is creepy with those dark drapes drawn," Nancy remarked.

"Kitty, kitty, kitty," Dora called. Three cats jumped down from the worn sofa and rubbed against her ankles.

"Charlotte is the big orange one, the long-haired blue is Emily. She's part Persian." Picking up the gray cat, she cooed, "And this is Little Lord Byron."

"They're sure glad to see yah," Molly said.

"Doesn't he have the cutest little pink nose," Dora cooed.

"Do they always make such a racket?" Nancy asked.

"That's their way of greeting me," Dora explained, kneading the soft gray fur. "Cats aren't as independent as they say. You know cats are..."

Nancy interrupted, "Let's get started, can I help you pack, Dora?"

"No, I'm not taking very much, I think I can manage." Dora started up the staircase. "Maybe you could get the cat carrying cases. They're in the hall closet."

Molly gazed at the high beamed ceiling. Her eyes followed Dora up the stairs. Holding out her arm, she nudged Nancy. "Look I got goose bumps.

To think they found Flora up there." She pointed at the stairs.

"Calm down, Molly, this house is very secure with those dead bolts on the front door." Her brow knit. "I wonder how a burglar managed to break in?"

"Who knows," Molly answered. "This place gives me the willies. I hope Dora hurries."

Thc closet door squeaked as Nancy pulled it open. Hanging in the front was one of the "Power of Poetry" jackets.

"Do you want your jacket?" Nancy yelled.

"She can't hear you, just take it," Molly advised. "Is poor Flora's jacket there too?"

"No, only this one. It looks small, maybe it's Flora's"?

"Then leave it, we don't want to upset Dora with more memories."

Nancy placed the jacket back on the wire hangar and grabbed a large cardboard case. "Kitty Traveler" was printed on its side.

"Come on cats," she called.

Hearing the sound of her voice, the cats scattered.

"Molly, can you help me get these animals?"

"Come on kitty, be a nice kitty." Molly cooed creeping closer to the orange cat. It sprang away, jumping on the edge of a table. It hissed as she came nearer.

"Maybe I can get the little one? She circled the room, case in her hand.

Nancy watched. "It's futile, the minute you get close, they run away."

"I'll get them," Dora announced, stepping down the stairs.

Nancy peered at the small overnight bag Dora toted. "Are you sure that's enough?"

"For me it's enough. I can always come back for anything I need. O.K., now for the cats, come on Emily and Charlotte. Get into your box like good girls."

Nancy and Molly watched speechless as the cats obeyed.

"See, look, Lord Byron is following them right in." Dora snapped the latch.

"They certainly mind you," Nancy gazed at Dora with new respect.

"You just have to know how to handle them." Dora said smiling smugly. "Don't let me forget their food."

On her way into the kitchen, she called, "Somebody will have to help me with this."

Nancy and Molly loaded the cartons filled with cans of "Kitty Delight" into the rear of the Land Rover.

"And there's the kitty litter, too," Dora reminded them.

"I didn't realize cats needed so many things," Molly said, carrying two large bags of litter.

Dora giggled. "They have more stuff than people do." She glanced down at the box in her arms. "These are their toys."

They squeezed into the front seat as Dora started the engine. "I sure appreciate you letting me stay with you, Molly."

As the car rolled down the hill, Nancy fumbled with the radio. "Let's see if we can hear any news about the burglary. Maybe they caught him."

Dora grunted, "I think they would let me know if they arrested somebody."

"Shhh, just listen."

"An unidentified man's body was discovered in the elevator at Darrel Place by one of the tenants last night. The victim had multiple stab wounds" The announcer continued. "Police have no clues to date. Stay tuned for..."

"My God!" Nancy exclaimed, "that's where Grayson lives."

"Stabbed just like Flora," Dora sobbed.

"Maybe we should phone Grayson when we get home" Molly suggested.

- 19 -

"You can take the spare room," Molly told Dora. "Pepper is using Leon's old room. Now all three bedrooms will be fillcd for a change."

"I'll just leave the cats in here for a minute," Dora said, placing the case beside the couch.

"O.K., now just follow me.

In the hall they passed Pepper talking to Leon on the hall phone.

Molly frowned, "She calls him long distance every fifteen minutes."

Pepper gave a feeble wave.

"My phone bill," Molly whispered, "is gonna' be more than the national debt,"

"Oh, this is nice," Dora said as Molly led her into the back bedroom. "It's all decorated in my favorite color, pink."

It's a lot cheerier than her room at that monastery she calls home, Molly thought. "You just put your things away, I'll be in the living room."

Passing Pepper in the hall, Molly checked her watch. Won't she ever get off that phone?

Molly was peering in the cat case when Dora entered the living room.

"I better get them settled first," she said, "Molly, where do you want me to put their litter box?"

Molly frowned, she had forgotten about that. "Maybe off the kitchen in the pantry."

"Out you come kitties, I'll fix you dinner."

"Come on, Molly and watch them eat."

Glancing at the hall, Molly shook her head. Oh dear, what had she got herself into?

- 20 -

Later that afternoon, Molly brow wrinkled. "I forgot to call Grayson about that newscast."

Dora, sitting on the other end of the sofa was too occupied playing with the three cats in her lap to answer. Molly groaned, listening to her.

"Pretty kitty," Dora cooed.

She hasn't heard a thing I've said, Molly thought. I'll test her. "I've phoned Grayson and he's off to the Antarctic for a vacation."

"Good," Dora held a furry paw. "Emily, can you learn how to shake hands?"

She hasn't heard a thing I've said, that woman's brain is full of cats.

Molly rolled her eyes toward the ceiling, hearing Pepper coo, "Goodbye, Leon, my dearest." Between the two of them, she glanced at Dora, still entranced, stroking Emily, they're driving me nuts.

"You know, Mom," Pepper said, rushing into the living room. "I've decided to return to Leon."

Molly peered at her daughter-in-law. "I'm happy for you, but what made you change your mind?"

The orange cat rubbed against Pepper's ankles. She reached for her. "Isn't she pretty?"

Dora smiled. "You like my Charlotte, dear?"

Pepper nodded. "Leon and I will get a cat.

"They're very soothing, great therapeutic treatment "Stroking their fur, is 'spose to lower blood pressure," Dora said.

"That's all well and good, but what's this about going back to Leon?" Molly asked.

Pushing her lower lip into a pout, Pepper admitted, "He's right after all. I didn't tell you, but I got a letter from the TV people today. Leon was right, they made a mistake. It wasn't my foot in the commercial."

"Who foot was it?" Dora asked.

"It doesn't matter anymore," Pepper gazed down at her sneakers. "Leon knew all along it wasn't the Finkel foot."

"I must phone Grayson," Molly announced, rising from her chair. She pressed the familiar number.

Glancing toward the living room, she watched Pepper and Dora. They had a toy mouse extended from a string. They gushed, making oohing sounds as the cats batted the toy.

"Somebody's gonna' have to tell poor Dora, Molly whispered into the receiver. "No, she can't hear me...the phone's in the hall, and she's too busy playing with her cats. Tell me, are you sure it was Donald..." Molly nodded, hanging up without saying goodbye.

"How's Grayson?" Dora patted the orange cat's head.

"Here let me take one," Molly offered, picking up the blue Persian.

"Sweet aren't they, Mom? Listen, you've got her little motor running."

Molly knit her brow, stroking the soft blue fur. How am I gonna' break it to Dora? I know, she thought. "What about we all go out for dinner tonight?"

"Count me out," Pepper blurted. "I promised to call Leon in a couple of hours."

Dora's eyes sparkled. "That would be kinda fun."

Good, Molly nodded. We go out and then I tell her after we have a good meal, of course. Molly closed her eyes. Now, what do I say? Grayson thinks it was Donald murdered on the elevator. Maybe I should invite Nancy? She could help me. She's good at breaking bad news. "That's a shame you can't join us," Dora said to Pepper. Turning toward Molly, she asked. "Are yah gonna' ask Nancy?"

It's as if she read my mind. Molly carried the blue Persian and released it on Dora's ample lap. "I'll phone her now."

Tweaking Charlotte's ear, Dora murmured, "You like it here, don't you pretty kitty?"

Molly raised her voice to be heard above the purrs echoing through the living room. "I tried to persuade her to come with us, but she's gonna' go to her ceramics class tonight. She's determined to make another jug."

Dora frowned. "I hope she doesn't give it to me. Her last one was terrible."

"Yeah, she doesn't have talent for pottery, she should stick to poetry. Grayson claims she has a real flair."

"She does write some beautiful verses. But may I confide in you, Molly?"

Molly bobbed her head as the small gray cat jumped into her lap. "Nice little Lord," she murmured.

"Sometimes I don't understand her poetry at all."

"Yeah, me too." Molly admitted. "How about we go to Chinatown. I haven't had Chinese food for a long time. See what you're missing, Pepper."

Pepper grinned, displaying her even teeth, and retreated to the hall.

"That girl has a beautiful smile," Dora said.

"Pepper," Molly called, "You're not gonna' phone Leon again?"

There was no answer.

"Oh, let her Molly, she's in love."

"But I pay the phone bill," Molly protested.

"Goodbye pretty kitties," Dora made soft clicking noises at the cats as she pulled her coat on.

Molly waved, "We'll see you later, kitties." I've never spoken to cats before. Dora sure got me doin' strange things.

- 21 -

"Gee, I thought they'd never leave," Pepper, muttered grabbing her coat from the closet. Checking the Muni schedule, she slammed the front door on her way out. Just wait until Molly hears about my psychic abilities. She'll really have something to brag about to her friends. Riding on the bus through the park, she rationalized. I am doing the right thing. Poor Molly, so depressed. It's that poetry group she joined. Weird people involved in a murder. "Your name," asked the desk Sergeant.

"Pepper Finkel, I had an appointment with Detective Merkel."

The Sergeant, turned, grinning at another officer. He faced Pepper, his face somber again. "So you're the physic, huh?"

"I'm the seventh daughter of a seventh daughter and possess unexplained powers."

"Yeah, well Detective Merkel, he paused spotting Dusty gesturing in the hallway. He tried to keep from laughing as he read Dusty's lips.

"Get rid of that crackpot."

"There's Detective Merkel," he pointed.

"Thank you," Pepper said, marching down the hall.

"You're the psychic who phoned?" Dusty acknowledged, covering his mouth with a hand to suppress his smile.

Pepper walked by him. "Is this your office?" she asked, sitting in a chair.

"I'm afraid Miss..."

"I have a personal interest in this case," Pepper interrupted. "Flora Stromboli was a dear friend of my mother, I mean my mother-in-law, Molly Finkel."

"Hmmm," Dusty scratched the stubble on his chin.

"They were in Grayson Crown's poetry group."

Retrieving a thick folder from the file cabinet, Dusty asked, "What else do you know about this case?"

"Well, I know that Grayson accused Flora of pushing Darla off the balcony. That upset my mom."

"He did?" Dusty drummed his pen on the desk. "Go on."

Though I never met Flora, I know her sister. In fact Dora Stromboli is staying with us now."

Dusty nodded. "What else do you know?"

"Well, I had this vision."

"Vision?" Dusty's eyebrows rose a whole inch.

"Psychics often see things in visions. I was eating cornflakes this morning. It was so clear, there was a red-haired man wielding a knife."

"You saw this?"

"I can described him," Pepper volunteered. "He was wearing a green plaid shirt and beige riding jodhpurs. He had a pencil-thin mustache that matched his hair.

"Did he look familiar?"

"Oh no, he was only a vision."

"That's interesting, Ma'am, but. The phone rang. "Be right there."

He studied Pepper. She was looking out the window. "Thanks, he whispered into the mouthpiece for rescuing me. into the mouthpiece "Sorry," he said, hanging up the receiver, "but have to investigate another stabbing. You don't have any vision of this one, do you?"

Pepper shook her head. "No, look I was just trying to help."

- 22 -

The Land Rover merged into the traffic on Grant Avenue. Molly gazed out the window at the small shops on both sides of the narrow street.

"Look!" she nudged Dora's elbow. "That place on the corner, The Topaz Dragon Cafe. There's a sign out in front. It says 'Dim Sum, special tonight, for only $2.50.' What's Dim Sum, Dora?"

"I don't know, but for $2.50 we can't go wrong. Let's eat there. I can pull in that garage next to the restaurant."

"Oh," Molly gasped reading the parking rates posted in front. "That garage is expensive."

"So, it doesn't matter because we can eat so cheap."

"Yes, we can afford to be extravagant." Molly fidgeted with her seat belt. After a nice meal, I can break it to her gently. It's better that way than seeing her dead Donald on television. Molly sighed, thinking, on a full stomach, she'll be able to handle it.

A garage attendant helped Dora and Molly out. Jumping in, he gunned the Land Rover's motor. Dora groaned, watching him head up the ramp. "He must be going 90."

"Don't worry," Molly advised, "he's a professional. Isn't it nice he offered to park your car."

Dora cringed hearing brakes screech from the upper level.

"Come on," Molly took her arm, leading her out of the garage.

A svelte lady clad in an electric-blue gown bowed to them as they entered the restaurant. Pulling two menus from the stack on the counter, she spoke in broken English. "Do you wish a table for two?"

"What is that Dim Sum?" Molly asked as she sank into the cushioned seat of a corner booth.

"Ah, a little bit of everything. You can try all our dishes, and see what you like."

"Tell me, is it only $2.50?"

The woman grinned. "Special tonight, Dim Sum is $2.50."

"That's a good gimmick," Dora whispered to Molly. "The samples are cheap, then the next time you eat here, you know what to order."

A waiter with a flame-colored dragon spiraling down the right side of his satin costume bowed. "Have you ladies decided?"

"I used to have lounging pajamas just like those," Dora giggled.

"Look at his long pigtail," Molly whispered, it makes me feel like I'm in China."

"Ladies, you want to order?"

"We'll have the special."

"Ah, Dim Sum very good."

"We also need forks," Dora reminded him. "You don't eat with chop-sticks, do yah, Molly?"

"No, Nancy is the one who can eat with those sticks. Once we went out for lunch and she insisted I use them. She showed me how to hold them, but when I raised the food to my mouth, it dropped off. I was hungry when we finished."

Scanning the ceiling, Dora squealed, "Look at all those cute hanging lanterns."

"Let's pretend we're in Hong Kong." Molly said watching Dora smile. She looks so happy. How clever I was suggesting this place. After a good dinner of that Dim Sum, breaking the news about Donald's tragic death will be easier.

Placing several small steaming bowls on the table, the waiter announced, "Dim Sum, very hot. More will come. You try?"

The women plunged spoons in the small bowls scooping portions of food on their dinner plates.

Dora sniffed, "I can smell lemon. I think it's the chicken."

"Mmmmmm," Molly murmured. "Try this Dora, I think it's shrimp with almonds."

Dora pushed a bowl toward Molly. "This one has cashews." Rolling a tea cart full of small bowls up to the table, the waiter asked, "Would you care for some?"

"Sure," Molly wet her lips. "Is that Dim Sum, too? Put it all on the table. Isn't this fun, Dora?"

Dora nodded, her mouth full. She swallowed. "You'd think they'd have larger tables with all these bowls."

"Yeah," Molly began eating faster. "We'd better hurry up, he's bringing that tea-cart again. Can you imagine, all of this for only $2.50?"

"Do you think Dim Sum would be a good theme for a poem?"

"Oh, Dora, how creative," Molly filled her dinner plate again.

Biting into a won ton, Dora chewed while she said. "This is a real bargain, Molly. I'm so glad you suggested this place."

"The tea-cart is rolling this way again." Molly picked up the centerpiece, a vase with five pink carnations. "We don't need this anymore," she told the waiter. "Just put one of those bowls there."

She advised Dora. "We'd better hurry and eat this. There's no room for anymore on this table."

Gripping an egg roll in each hand, Dora answered, I'm doin' my best."

"Food all O.K.?" the waiter asked.

"I still can't believe we get all this for $2.50." Molly answered.

The waiter bowed, his pigtail bobbing. "Yes each bowl $2.50."

Color drained from Molly's face. "Stop!" she screamed. "Dora don't eat another bite."

"What?" Dora dropped her fork on a mound of rice.

"Didn't yah hear him, each of these little bowls is $2.50."

"What," Dora choked.

"Quick put all the food we haven't touched in this corner." Molly's hand trembled as she grabbed bowls.

Dora waved to the waiter.

"Everything O.K.?" he asked.

"There's been a mistake, we want to return all these dishes we haven't eaten." Molly blurted.

"Food not good?"

"Food fine, price wrong." Molly pointed to the bowls. "Each one of these are $2.50?"

"Ah," he nodded. "Everything $2.50 each."

"Oh my," Dora gulped. "Our bill's gonna' be over two hundred dollars."

"Oh, bill," the waiter grinned, rubbing his hands together. "You ladies want bill. I get now."

Dora fumbled in her large purse. "I've got my credit card here somewhere."

"Good," Molly released a deep breath. "At least we won't have to wash dishes. I'll pay my share when we get home."

Pouring the remaining tea into Molly's cup, Dora advised. "Relax, drink up, we paid for it."

Molly held the cup to her lips. "Guess I better tell you now." She blurted. "Grayson says the dead man he found in the elevator is your Donald."

Dora's face turned an ashen color. She didn't answer.

"Of course, Molly stammered, "the police haven't identified the body yet...maybe Grayson is wrong It could be someone else."

Dora rose from the table. "I have to go to the ladies room."

"Dora are you O.K.?" Molly asked, following her.

"I think I'm gonna' throw up."

Molly stood hugging the basin listening to retching and gagging sounds behind the closed stall.

She mumbled, "Over a hundred dollars of delicacies down the toilet."

- 23 -

The blue Persian rubbed against Molly's ankle, purring. Reaching down, she stroked its soft fur. "Dora will feed you soon, Kitty." Here it is Friday morning and I need to write a poem. My mind is a blank. How can I think with all the excitement around here. I can't blame Dora and Pepper, but they are disruptive to my creativity.

There was a knock at the front door. The cat arched his back before fleeing into the kitchen. "Coming, coming." Molly muttered.

"Nancy, what are you doin' here so early?"

"Brought you something," she said, handing Molly a box with a yellow bow on top. "I finished it yesterday."

Ruffling through layers of tissue paper, Molly asked. "What could this be?." She pulled out a teal-colored jug.

Nancy smiled. "It's for your mantle."

Molly set the jug next to the photo. Stepping back, she gazed at the display. Before she could speak, Pepper entered the living room, duffel bag under her arm.

"What that?" Pepper asked.

"Nancy made it for me."

Pepper yawned. "It's lopsided."

"Shhhhh," Molly pressed a finger against her lip.

"I knew it," Nancy blared.

Molly glared at Pepper, "It looks O.K. to me."

Slumping on the sofa, Pepper rested her feet on the coffee table. "I'm leaving this morning. The airport limo is going to pick me up."

Molly whispered a silent prayer. "Then everything's O.K. between you and Leon?"

"Yeah, I just need space, but I miss Leon, and I'm anxious to see the kids. They're coming home this weekend. Pepper gazed down at her sneakers. "I should confess, I sent the boys to that camp because they were getting too hard to handle. You were right, Mom, I've been too lax with them."

Nancy tilted her head, still studying her handiwork. "You're a very lucky woman having two sons."

"Another thing," Pepper knitted her brow. "Leon's worried with all those killings. He'd like you to come, too." She hesitated. I better not tell her that my psychic ability didn't work this time.

"It's nice that Leon cares about me, but I'll be O.K. here with Dora and the cats."

"Is Dora sick?" Pepper asked. "I heard her moaning last night." Nancy turned toward Molly, "You told her about Donald."

Molly nodded.

Patting Molly's shoulder, Nancy said, "Grayson told me that Darla, Flora and Donald all had strands of black hair on their hands. Detective Merkel thinks it belongs to the killer."

As a psychic, I stink, Pepper thought.

"Then it couldn't be one of us," Molly sighed.

"Dora's hair is dark," Nancy reminded her, "But it isn't black."

"There's somethin' strange with Dora though." "What do you mean?" Nancy asked, moving her jug to the other side of the mantel. Perhaps it won't look so lop-sided away from the photo?

"Well, for one thing, she's never home, except to feed those cats."

"Could be she feels she's imposing on you, Molly."

"No, she gets these phone calls all the time, and she's off somewhere. She never tells me where. Then there's all those clothes she's buying."

"Yes," Pepper agreed. "Everyday she comes home with another new outfit."

"She may just need a life. After all, she's had a terrible tragedy."

"But she never wears anything new. She keeps those department store boxes stacked in her room."

"You know, when Alan died, I acted a little strange. Didn't want to see anyone or do anything. I was becoming a hermit...until," Nancy bit her lip. "I have a confession to make."

Molly's eyes widened. "Everybody has confessions this morning."

"I phoned Darla Rhodes for advice."

"That's nothin', so did I," Molly admitted.

"It was a rainy afternoon," Nancy went on, "I rationalized half the Bay Area watches, so I didn't give my right name."

"You don't have to even tell your name." Molly interrupted. "What was Darla's advice?"

"She was instrumental in steering me toward Grayson's class. Well, not exactly, first I joined the ceramic group."

"Where you made that jug," Pepper giggled, looking out the window.

"I found poetry suited me more."

"Yeah, you're a good poet, Nancy. You write some beautiful things."

"There he is," Pepper cried, spotting a white limo pulling up at the curb. "Well, I'm off." She pressed her lip against Molly's cheek.

"Thanks for everything, Mom. And, if you change your mind about coming, phone."

Peeking through the blinds, Molly watched the driver open the car door for Pepper. She cringed. Underneath the chauffeur's cap, strands of coarse black hair flowed to his shoulders.

- 24 -

"Mondays," Grayson muttered. watching the parade of cars on the Bay Bridge. Bumper to bumper already and it's only, he checked his watch, 2 p.m.

"Right on time, ladies," he announced as Molly and Nancy marched into the living room.

"Where's Dora?" Grayson peered down the hall. "Is she all right? You did break it to her about Donald?"

"She took it pretty well, considering," Molly said, sitting on the lemon-colored couch. "I think I should have picked a better time to tell her, though. She went down to file some more papers."

"She's still trying to have Flora's body released so she can arrange the funeral." Nancy added.

"Poor thing," Molly shook her head. "She really didn't feel like listening to poetry today."

Nancy joined Molly on the couch. "As if any of us are in the mood."

Observing their pained expressions, Grayson said, "Poetry is a wonderful release for the emotions."

He pushed the wooden podium to the center of the room. "Is something else wrong?"

"It's our jackets," Molly whined. "We can't find them anywhere."

"I spent all morning searching for mine." Nancy's brow wrinkled. "I always hang it in the hall closet, but it disappeared."

"That's odd," Grayson carried in the coffee urn. "Is Dora's missing, too?"

Before Nancy could answer, the doorbell chimed.

"Hi Gray," Bunny nodded to Molly and Nancy, as she plopped down in the wing chair facing them.

"Nancy and Molly's poetry jackets are missing." Grayson announced.

"I have mine on, see." Bunny rose from the chair and slowly turned. "Since all this happened, I thought black was appropriate today." She stroked her black pants. "The jacket goes well with these, don't you think?"

"Very color coordinated," Grayson answered. "Strange things are happening with those jackets. I can't figure it out." His features relaxed. "Shall we get on with the poetry reading?"

"Let's," Bunny blurted, removing her jacket and draping it on the chair back.

"May I see that for a minute?"

Bunny handed her jacket to him."

Turning the garment inside out, Grayson examined the lilac-colored lining. "Looks in tack."

"Everything all right?" Bunny asked as Grayson handed the jacket back to her.

"Fine, does anyone have a poem to read?"

"I do, Gray, I finally finished my ode. I renamed it 'Tribute To Ecstasy." Bunny's hips wiggled as she slinked to the center of the room.

Pausing, she cleared her throat before placing a pink sheet of paper on the podium. She began, glancing up after reading each line.

"My God," gasped Nancy, "that's obscene."

Molly gazed down at her shoes, her face flushed. "She shouldn't read things like that."

"I can't believe this." Nancy's palm covered her mouth. She's describing male genitalia in rhyme." Molly's mouth gaped open.

"Why doesn't Grayson stop her, Nancy wondered?

Squirming, Molly closed her eyes. This is too embarrassing. Suddenly Bunny was silent.

"Thank God, I think she's finished," Nancy whispered to Molly.

"Well what do yah think?" Bunny's eyes darted around the room.

"Doesn't anyone want to critique me?"

Fumbling with her handbag, Molly pretended to search for an unknown object. She peeked at Grayson.

He sat very still, his head lowered gazing at an invisible spot on his shoe.

Nancy stared out the window.

Someone has to say somethin," Molly thought. "Very nice," she commented. "The rhythm was good."

"Couldn't you find another topic?" Nancy snapped. "That was pure porn, disgusting."

Tapping his fingers on the coffee table, Grayson said, "Interesting, In my opinion, your piece is beyond critique."

Nancy glared at Bunny. "It's indecent, you should be censored."

"Now ladies," Grayson wiped his brow with a white handkerchief. He stepped up to the podium, standing beside Bunny. "We never want to censor our work. Censorship is dangerous to the arts. Let's remember to keep open minds. If censorship prevailed, who knows where it would end. Our creative efforts must remain free."

"Well, the rhymes were good," Molly said, ignoring Nancy's glare.

The phone ringing interrupted any further comments.

Thank God, Nancy thought.

The women watched Grayson as he held the receiver and nodded.

"Something wrong, Gray?" Bunny asked, as he hung up.

"That was Dusty Merkel. I asked him to notify me if there were any further developments. I was right, the police have a positive identification of the body. It was Donald Palmcroft."

"Poor Dora," Molly moaned, "She still hoped that it wasn't her Donald." She took a sip of coffee.

"But at least you prepared her," Nancy said. "That's better than hearing it on the news."

Bunny's eyes widened. "Why was she so concerned, he was Darla's boyfriend now?"

Leaning back on the sofa, Molly explained. "Dora was still in love with him. I'm grateful she couldn't come today."

Bunny gazed out the window at the stream of cars crossing the bridge. "It's going to be tough on her when she finds out he transferred his affections to Darla Rhodes."

"The police believe," Grayson pointed to the ceiling, "he was living up there with her. But, of course, I knew that."

Bunny faced Molly and Nancy. "That Donald was nothing but a spineless fortune hunter. The way that man used women. It doesn't surprise me at all that someone killed him. Dora should feel lucky she's free of that louse."

"Oh, Bunny," Molly shook her index finger. "You shouldn't speak that way about the dead."

"How do you know so much about this Donald?" Nancy asked, gulping the rest of her coffee.

"His reputation travels fast. Besides I'm only being honest."

"Have some more coffee, ladies," Grayson suggested. "Let's discuss next week's assignment. He refilled Bunny's cup, frowning at her. Why doesn't she keep her mouth closed?

"Do the police think Donald Palmcroft was involved with Flora's death?" Nancy inquired.

"Dusty won't reveal too much about the case to me, however, he did let out that they found the same blood samples at Flora's and in the elevator."

"What about the black hair?" Nancy asked, taking another sip of her coffee.

"Yes, they're investigating that, too."

"Oh dear," Molly moaned. "And what about poor Darla, do the police believe someone pushed her?"

"I have something to show you." Grayson strode into the bathroom, opened the hamper and flung the contents on the tile floor. "Where is it?" he cried.

“Where’s what, Gray?” Bunny stood by the door, watching him examine the pile of towels on the floor. “What are you looking for?”

“It was here, wrapped in a blue towel,” Grayson groaned. Why didn’t I turn it over immediately to Dusty? I didn’t tell you, but I discovered a small scrap of satin. That Donald guy had a death-grip on it. Looked just like the lining to our poetry jackets.”

“Are you sure?” Nancy peered at him with disbelief.

“I’m sure,” he muttered. “Why did I hide it?”

“Taking it, makes you an accessory to murder, doesn’t it.” Nancy said, studying Grayson’s face.

“I don’t know, but I just wanted to protect you ladies. There’s nothing I can do now, it’s gone.”

“You wanted to protect us, that’s sweet, Grayson.” Molly patted his arm.

“Thanks, Molly. When I found that purple ‘P’ at Darla’s I was sure Flora had something to do with it. She was the only one who didn’t wear her jacket, and no one else had a ‘P’ missing.”

“I didn’t tell you, but Flora phoned me that night and said she knew who pushed Darla off the balcony. Someone stabbed her before she told me. I wish now I had leveled with Dusty from the start.”

Nancy dropped her cup on the saucer. “Well I hope you don’t think Molly or I had anything to do with this because our jackets are missing.”

“Or me,” Bunny flung her jacket over her shoulders. “But then I have my jacket. Say Gray, what about the blood found at Flora’s and in the elevator?”

“Detective Merkel said the samples belonged to the same person.”

“Whoever killed those two must have a nasty cut.” Bunny snickered.

"Oh my God! Molly exclaimed! "Dora had a bandage on her arm. She told me one of the cats scratched her. I forgot which one."

Pulling up her sleeve, Nancy displayed a small plastic bandage on her arm. "See, I have one too. Gashed myself on a broken piece of pottery."

"As long as we're playing show and tell." Bunny rolled up one of her pants legs. "Heartly and I were romping and he gave me a little love nip on my leg."

"Let's not confess all at once," Grayson said, turning toward Molly. "And what about you, any suspicious wounds?"

Scanning her arms, Molly frowned. "No, nothing, I'm always left out of everything."

- 25 -

Molly slammed the front door. Hanging her coat in the closet, she probed among the other garments. That poetry jacket must be here. I always hang it when I come back. Wouldn't wear it any other place except Grayson's.

She scanned the closet floor. Maybe it fell off the hanger?" She abandoned her search hearing four bells from the clock. Time for Darla's show, she thought.

Flipping the switch on the television, she suddenly remembered, Darla won't be on anymore.

"Pack up your troubles," started playing in the background, but the screen read: "The Advice From Audrey Show." A woman with obviously hennaed hair sat in Darla's familiar red chair. "Hump," Molly emitted, her hair color and that chair clash.

She grinned glad to see Audrey so uncomfortable with Darla's props. "You'd think they'd change the set," she muttered.

That Audrey, Molly shook her head. What a phony smile. She couldn't advise anyone. Frowning, Molly watched the screen. Audrey picked up Darla's blue telephone. Some anonymous woman was sobbing at the other end. "My husband is having an affair with his secretary," she whined.

"Why do you suspect that?" Audrey asked, pretending to act concerned.

"There were large amounts drawn from our checking account made out to..."

"Don't say the name," Audrey snapped.

"Well they were made out to a local jewelry store. The only present my husband bought me was a steam iron," the woman wept. "And that was two years ago."

Audrey made clicking noises with her tongue.

Ah, Molly nodded. That's exactly what Darla would do.

"Now," Audrey cleared her throat, "What do you base your assumptions on?"

"Stupid," Molly shouted at the TV, she just told you, Audrey."

Audrey stammered, "You must confront your husband, tell him you're aware of what's going on. If you love your husband, try counseling."

"No, no," Molly groaned. That's not what Darla would advise. "Pack your bag and leave that two-timer. But before you do, stop at that jewelry store and buy yourself an expensive trinket. Remember, charge it to your husband's account." Yeah, that's what Darla would say.

That Audrey she's gushing now, spending too much time with one caller. Probably because there's no one waiting on the phone.

What was this? Molly tuned up the volume. The voice of the troubled woman sounded belligerent.

"Thanks, but no thanks, I'll take my own advice." A click interrupted the conversation. Molly chuckled as the camera zoomed in on Audrey's bewildered face. She doesn't know what to do now?

Darla knew how to handle people. I'll never call that Audrey for advice.

The hall phone rang. Walking to the phone, Molly kept her eyes focused on the screen. Can you believe that Audrey is giving a monologue on how dedicated she is. Guess she figures she has to convince more people to call.

"I'm coming, I'm coming,: Molly shouted to the phone.

She picked up the receiver, "Yes?...Dora is that you?...Where are you?...O.K. I'll feed them."

Hanging up the receiver, she glanced at the screen, Audrey was still speaking. Enough of her, Molly thought switching off the television.

She peered under the sofa, calling, "Kitty, kitty. Why couldn't she remember their names.? She scratched her salt and pepper hair. Weren't they named after dead writers or something?"

"Kitty, kitty, Charlotte," ah that was right, now who was the orange one? "Elizabeth, is that your name, Kitty?"

"That little gray one meowed at her. Now what was his name? "Lord?" she hesitated, Lord Somebody, come with me into the kitchen."

Retrieving their special yellow bowls from the cupboard, she assured herself, when they smell their food, they'll come.

The cat food was still packed in the carton. There wasn't enough cupboard space for all those cans. Bending down, she grabbed three cans of "Kitty Delight."

Now what is this? She dislodged a small receipt clinging to the bottom of a can.

Placing it on the sideboard by the sink, she slid each can under the electric opener. She scooped equal amounts of the mix in each bowl.

"Phu, smells awful." I wonder how they eat this stuff. Looking down she saw three pair of emerald eyes watching her. My goodness, their quiet, I didn't even hear them sneak in.

"O.K., come on cats, I'm sorry but I can't remember your names." She placed the bowls on the comic sheet from the Sunday paper.

Purring noises made Molly smile. Those cats are kind of cute after all. I'll have to ask Dora again what their names are.

She was about to throw the receipt in the garbage when she paused.

Maybe this is important. Putting on her reading glasses, she studied the small scrap of paper. Cat food is sure expensive at Ralph's. Wait, she reminded herself, didn't Dora say she bought this at the All-Night Market? She studied the time and date, October 14th at 5:09 P.M. Why that was the day after Darla's death, the day they were over at Grayson's.

Poor Flora was still alive. Molly recalled how they told everyone they had to leave to buy cat food on the way home. But, Molly wondered, that's impossible?

She could still hear Dora's voice explaining how she ran out of cat food the night Flora was stabbed. "I had to go to the All-Night Market because I couldn't let them go hungry."

Molly's hands trembled clasping the receipt. Maybe I should show this to Nancy? Grabbing her coat, she headed next door.

"Who's there?" Nancy's voice blasted out of the speaker by the front gate.

"I must talk to you," Molly whispered, pressing her face close to the speaker.

The buzzer sounded, opening the gate.

"Now I may be wrong," Molly waved the receipt. "Didn't Dora say she was buying cat food the night it happened?"

"Yes, she said Flora was busy writing a poem and wouldn't go with her. Then she had a flat tire."

"Somethin's wrong," Molly said, handing Nancy the receipt. "Look at this."

"This is for cat food," Nancy said, scanning the scrap.

"But, it's from Ralph's and it's dated Friday afternoon."

Checking the date again, Nancy pondered. "That's odd, why did Dora lie to us?"

Molly clasped her hands together. "Do you think she had anything to do with Flora's death?"

"I don't know? I wonder why she would fabricate such a story?" Nancy rested her palm against her cheek. "And go into such details about the flat tire?"

"What else do you think she lied about?" Molly asked, "Maybe that story about the cat scratching her wasn't true either? You know Dora's hair is close to black."

"Relax, Molly, we're over reacting. Would you care for a cup of coffee?"

Without waiting for an answer, Nancy pushed the swinging dutch doors and disappeared into the kitchen.

"I'm going to make some for myself, so you might as well have a cup, too."

Molly rose from her seat on the couch. Standing in front of the window, the color drained from her face. "Oh, my God!"

Running from the kitchen, Nancy stood beside her. "What's wrong?"

Molly pointed to the Land Rover parking in front. "It's Dora, she just drove up and now she's going into my house."

"Molly, you gave her the key."

"Do you realize I may be living with a murderess?" Molly trembled. "Do you think we should call the police?"

"Think rationally, you ask Dora why she lied about going to the All-Night Market. There must be a reasonable explanation."

Clutching Nancy's shoulder, Molly asked, "Will you ask her?"

"Let's relax for a few minutes, have our coffee, then I'll go back with you and we'll get to the bottom of this. Calm down, Molly."

Molly returned to the couch. She gulped her coffee in silence.

Opening her purse, she pulled out a key ring and toyed with her house key.

"All right, let's go," Nancy said slipping on a blue sweater.

Molly lagged behind her as they neared the white stucco.

"Come on, Molly" Nancy urged. "It's your house. Don't be scared."

Before Molly inserted the key in the lock, the door swung open. "I saw you coming," Dora smiled, still carrying her tote bag. "Did you feed the cats?"

Molly didn't answer. She peered over Dora's head. "Everything looks O.K." she mumbled.

"Why wouldn't it?" Dora asked.

Nudging Nancy's elbow, Molly begged, "Show her, show her the receipt."

"Here," Nancy handed her the scrap.

Dora studied it. "Yes, that's a receipt for cat food. What's wrong?"

"Tell her," Molly pled. "to look at the date and time."

"I still don't know what you're talking about?" Dora flung her palms out exasperated.

"You lied to us about when you bought that cat food. Tell her, Nancy."

"There appears to be a discrepancy about your activities the night Flora was stabbed."

"I don't understand, you're making a big to do about a grocery receipt."

Molly's cheeks flushed, her eyes glared, "It isn't the date or time you told us. You lied!" Dora's mouth gaped.

"I don't know what else you lied about, but I want you to get out."

"Let's go inside and discuss this calmly," Nancy suggested. Planting her foot on the inside of the door, Molly pushed Dora outside. "We can discuss this right here."

"Please, just tell Molly where you were that night," Nancy asked. "I can't."

"I don't want you staying her, Molly cried. "I won't share my home with a lying murderess."

"Nancy, you tell her I'll get out right now." Dora pulled her car keys from the tote bag.

Nancy hesitated, before asking, "Why did you lie? I dislike taking sides, but I think you owe us an explanation."

A tear slid down Dora's cheek. "You're against me, too."

"Did you lie about the cat scratch?" Molly badgered. "You should go down to the police, they'd like a sample of your blood."

"Huh," Dora sobbed, turning to Nancy. "What's she talking about?"

Wiping a tear with her finger, she regained her composure. Marching toward the Land Rover, she shouted, "I won't stay with anyone who thinks I'm a murderess."

Molly and Nancy jumped as a loud backfire exploded. They watched as the Land Rover lurched from side to side rolling down the street.

"Molly, I think you acted too rash. Why didn't you give her a chance to explain?"

"Explain, and lie some more, I can't believe a thing that comes out of her mouth."

- 26 -

Weaving among the out-door tables at Enrico's Cafe, Grayson spotted an empty one. The fog arrested beyond the Golden Gate resulted in unseasonable sultry weather. Grayson sat down.

"What'll you have?" a black-vested waiter asked.

Grayson hesitated, checking his watch. Should I wait for her? She's always late. "I'm expecting a friend."

The waiter shrugged and started walking away.

"Wait," Grayson called. "On second thought, I'll have an Irish coffee."

Scanning the other tables, he smiled. Women attired in pastel-cotton dresses and white sandals conversing with their escorts sporting colorful short-sleeved shirts. Most had a camera around their neck.

Tourists, Grayson scoffed. They think they're in Hawaii. Won't they be surprised when a blanket of fog invades, and the temperature drops. Oh how they'll stampede back to their hotels for warmer clothing then.

"Hey Bunny," he waved. Blinking he noticed her navy-blue suit as she approached the table. Heads turned as she maneuvered her way between tables. Yes, she's still a very attractive woman. "You're in a conservative mood today?" he asked. "Gray," she murmured, sitting facing the interior of the cafe. She lit a king-sized cigarette.

Grayson frowned. "Must you?" He glared at the coil of smoke emitting from the burning tip.

Bunny exhaled, watching him cover his nose with a napkin. "Look, that's why I asked you to meet me here. We're out in the air and if I want to smoke, you shouldn't act so smart-assed."

Dropping the napkin, Grayson turned his head away from here. "I'll bear it. Now what's up?"

"I want to ask you a favor."

"So you told me on the phone."

"All of these killings," Bunny waved her cigarette. "It's just been too much for me. First, Charlie, and then the others." Grayson turned toward her, his hand covering his face. "Yes, it has been tough," He said, his voice muffled.

"The police don't even have a clue." A single tear glistened on her cheek. Pulling a tissue out of her purse, she dabbed her face. "I'm very depressed, Gray."

God, Grayson thought, she almost looks pathetic.

The waiter set the coffee down. "And what will you have, Miss?" "The same,"

Bunny answered, her eyes sweeping his lanky frame. "He's kinda cute," she whispered.

Grayson sipped his coffee. "Good," he mumbled under his breath as Bunny squashed the cigarette in an ashtray.

"What?" she asked.

"Tell me what you want?"

"Ricardo, you don't know him," Bunny paused pulling another cigarette out of her pack. "He was someone I met on a cruise to South America a couple of years ago."

"You're chain smoking." Grayson protested.

"Look I've got a lot on my mind," she said, lighting the cigarette.

"You remember the time Charlie and me had that terrible fight?"

"Yes, you were absent from my class for a few weeks." Grayson leaned away, dodging blasts of smoke.

"Can you believe Ricardo phoned me from Rio last night?" He wants me to come down there. Said he couldn't forget me." She took a deep drag.

"It's kinda nice being unforgettable.

"And, you're going"

"Sure," Bunny blew a wisp a smoke out of her nostrils.

"This is so sudden, have you given it much thought?"

The waiter interrupted, setting down Bunny's cup of Irish coffee.

"Here you are, Miss. Will there be anything else?"

"Well, since you asked," said Bunny, her eyes twinkling.

"No that will be all." Grayson glared at her. "Act your age."

"Oh, Gray, you're no fun at all."

"O.K., let's get back to Rio."

"I have nothing here," Bunny toyed with the her cup, "except Heartly. I don't want to board him in one of those impersonal kennels. You know he won't get any love or attention from strangers. Bunny ground her cigarette out. Grayson sighed.

"Poor Heartly," she cooed. His little heart will break and he might even get sick."

"Tragic," Grayson agreed.

"That's how I thought you'd feel, so I decided your the best person I can think of to take care of Heartly."

Grayson's eyebrows rose two inches, "Me?"

"Oh dear, you're not allergic to dogs?"

"Unfortunately no, just cats. There's something about their fur."

"Well Heartly doesn't have a furry coat, and there's no one else."

Bunny's eyes misted. "Nancy is too fussy about her house to allow animals.

Dora and all those mangy cats moved in with Molly. Heartly hates cats, so you have something in common."

Stroking his brow, Grayson wondered, how do I get out of this one? "Gray," Bunny pled,"You're the only person I trust to take care of Heartly. You'll see, he'll be good company."

Grayson pondered, sipping his coffee. Maybe she was right. The small white Italian Greyhound with the fawn heart on his side might make a good roommate. "He's housebroken?"

"Of course, he'll tell you when he needs to go out for a walk."

"How?"

Bunny ignored his question. "Now my flight leaves tomorrow at 6 p.m.

So, you can come over in the afternoon and pick him up. I'd drop him off at your place, but I'm going to be so busy packing and taking care of things. Do you realize I have to revamp my whole wardrobe? The seasons are opposite there, something to do with being on the other side of the equator."

"How long are you going to be away?"

"Who knows?" Bunny shrugged. "If I remember Ricardo had a special Latin charm, and now that I'm single, I'm going to have some fun for a change." "Aren't you being terribly impulsive?" Grayson asked, staring at his empty cup. Should he order another?

"Well, Bunny said, pulling out another cigarette, "You only live once."

Turning away from the stream of smoke, Grayson gazed at the traffic on Broadway. "Wait a minute!" he exclaimed. Isn't that Dora's Land Rover?"

"Where?" Bunny's eyes followed his.

"See," he pointed. "She stopped at that signal. Looks like she's crying." Standing up he shouted, "Dora, Dora, over here."

Patrons from adjoining tables glared at him.

"Sit down, Gray, she doesn't hear you."

The signal changed to green and the Land Rover turned up the hill.

"I think she might be heading toward my place."

"If you're worried about her, you can leave."

"It might be a good idea." Grayson motioned to the waiter. "The bill," he called. "Pathetic, that poor woman losing her sister and Donald too."

"I'll expect you tomorrow then, but not too early, I need my sleep."

"I'll be there." Grayson said.

- 27 -

Grayson spotted Dora hovering by his front door as he left the elevator. She grasped at his arm not letting him turn the key in the lock. "Oh, Grayson, I would have phoned. See," she held up a leather coin purse. I don't have any change." "O.K. Dora, relax. Let me open the door." She withdrew her arm. "Come in, tell me what's wrong." "Molly doesn't want me there anymore. She kicked me out." Dora seated herself in a straight-backed chair. Her fingers kneaded a torn tissue. "Oh, it's just too horrible. She thinks I murdered Flora. I think Nancy does too. What am I gonna' do?" Grayson reached for a glass under the bar. Pouring himself a straight Scotch, he peered at Dora. "Can I fix you a drink?" "Oh, I don't drink," Dora sniffled. "But do you have any tissues? I ran out, and my nose keeps running." "Wait, I'll get you a box." Grayson disappeared into the bathroom. "The trouble is they know I lied," she shouted after him. "You lied?" Grayson said, handing her a new box of tissues. His eyes strayed to the window. What was she talking about? A thick layer of fog wrapped around the Bay Bridge towers until they dissolved. "It's really coming in," Grayson said. Turning to face Dora, he asked. "What did you lie about?" "The night Flora died, I told them I was shopping for cat food, and about having a flat tire. That was my excuse for not getting back." Dora plunged her nose into the tissue. "Where were you?" Grayson sipped his Scotch, listening to the sound of Dora blowing her nose. "Your nose must be sore from all that rubbing."

"It is," Dora nodded.

"Where were you the night Flora was stabbed?"

"It's just so embarrassing to tell what really happened, Dora babbled, pulling out another tissue. You remember me talking about my Donald?"

"Donald Palmcroft," Grayson gulped his scotch. Pouring himself another drink, he said, "Your Donald was the man found murdered in the elevator? Didn't Molly tell you?"

"Poor Donald, Dora wailed.

"Yeah, Poor Donald," Grayson repeated. "I thought you ended that affair?"

"Now I realize he wasn't just my Donald, he was everyone's Donald. He was Bunny's Donald and Darla's Donald, and God knows who else's Donald.

That night Flora and I had a terrible argument about him. You know, he started phoning me again."

Grayson took a sip of his drink. "Go on, I'm listening."

"He sounded awful, so upset. He needed someone to talk to. How did I know that Flora was listening on the extension upstairs? He told me he knew who pushed Darla off the balcony."

Grayson drank the last of his Scotch. "Was Donald responsible for Darla's death?"

"Heavens, I didn't think so, but Flora did. That's what we argued about. She said I was crazy to date a murderer. I got so mad at her, I walked out. It was my fault the door was unlocked. I do feel responsible for Flora's death. If I knew how to lock that door, Flora would still be alive."

"Whoever broke in would have found another way. You shouldn't harbor guilt feelings, Dora."

Gazing at Grayson through puffy pink eyes, she asked, "You think so?"

"Flora phoned me that night, right before, claimed to have information about Darla's killer."

Dora wadded a tissue into a ball before she spoke. "Flora didn't know anything." Drawing out a fresh tissue, she wiped her nose. "She was absolutely sure Donald pushed Darla off that balcony. Heaven knows, I tried to convince her that Donald had nothing to do with it. You know, she wouldn't believe me."

"When you left that night, did you meet Donald?"

"He said he'd be waiting for me at this restaurant. It was at Fisherman's Wharf, 'The Sea Turtle.' They specialize in swordfish, and squid. I remember ordering swordfish. Squid just doesn't appeal to me. It wasn't very crowded because it was so late. I was already seated when Donald arrived. He looked terrible." Dora paused.

"Then what happened?" Grayson eyed the bottle of Scotch. No more, he thought, no matter what that woman says.

"Donald told me the guilt had finally caught up with him."

"Guilt?" Grayson asked, wondering how Dora managed such an endless stream of tears. The woman must certainly be dehydrated. "Are you sure you wouldn't like a cold drink?"

Dora shook her head. "Donald told me he had done something terrible a couple years ago." She wiped her eyes, throwing the wadded tissue in the wastebasket. "He wouldn't tell me what it was 'cause he said he wanted to protect me. You know, he asked me to marry him again." Dora's shoulders shook as she sobbed louder.

"Easy, easy," Grayson said.

"Donald told me he loved me, even the way I look with all this weight." Grayson, do you realize, I was almost a bride!"

Grayson nodded, thinking Dora did have a pretty face. Maybe Donald's interest was not her money.

"Donald told me he had to take care of some things before we eloped. I dreaded going home and facing Flora, so I drove around town most of the night. You can't imagine, Grayson, how horrible that was. There aren't too many places open, and there's hardly anyone on the streets."

"You don't think he went back to your house after he left you?"

"No, he was going to Darla's penthouse. He left a lot of his things there."

"Detective Merkel told me they found strands of black hair in the victim's hands. That lets Donald out, his hair was blond."

Rolling her bloodshot eyes, Dora wailed. "How could I tell Molly and Nancy?"

"You don't think they'd understand?"

"After I moved in with Molly, I began shopping for my trousseau. I kept it a secret."

"Maybe the police are right suspecting a burglar broke into your house."

Dora reached for another tissue. "I don't know? Nothing was missing, even Flora's money was still there. She kept it all over the house in jars and drawers, and even some bills under her mattress." Dora sobbed, "She always said, 'it'll take a burglar so damn long to find it, he'd give up.' You know, she was right, it took me almost an hour to check, and I knew all her hiding places."

"Detective Merkel believes Flora frightened whoever broke in and he panicked."

"Somebody murdered Donald and now we can never marry." Tears flowed from her eyes. "I thought I'd be Mrs. Donald Palmcroft, and now I'll never be a Mrs. anybody."

Grayson placed his empty glass on the bar. This is the wrong time to get snockered. "It's odd Flora phoned me."

"That's because you thought she did it. You shouldn't have accused her."

Gazing out at the bridge, Grayson noticed how sparse the traffic was. He checked his watch. "It's getting late, Dora. Do you want to stay over tonight?"

Dora face flushed as she stared at her shoes.

Oh, good God, what is she thinking? "What I meant is," he tried to explain. "You certainly can't go back to Molly's.

"I don't want to go home either."

"Look, I have a spare bedroom and can even loan you some pajamas."

"You know Molly threatened to call the police if I didn't leave. She pointed to three faint marks on her plump arm. "See these! Molly didn't believe Emily scratched me. Emily has a nasty temper sometimes."

Grayson touched her arm. "Looks like scratches to me. Come on, Dora," He said, escorting her toward the spare room. "Imagine, Molly wants me to go and have my blood tested. Do you know why?"

Grayson didn't answer. He pulled a folded pair of green plaid pajamas from the bureau drawer. "These may fit."

"That's nice of you," she said, her face turning crimson, but I don't wear men's things."

"I'll leave them on the bed. Tomorrow I'll phone Molly and straighten this out."

Dora moaned, "Oh dear, I guess there's not much choice, I have to sleep somewhere."

- 28 -

The mid-morning sun penetrated a thick bank of fog shining through Grayson's bedroom window. His eyes opened to look at the clock on the nightstand.

He sat up in bed. His head throbbed. Too much Scotch, he thought, or maybe it was listening to the snoring and sobbing from the spare room. How that woman could do both at the same time was amazing.

I have plenty of time. Bunny didn't expect him until afternoon.

Better wear a robe this morning. Don't want to shock Dora. He tiptoed out of his bedroom. Passing the spare room, he paused, listening. It's quiet. She's probably still asleep.

Plugging in the coffee-maker, he waited in the living room. What am I going to do about Dora, he wondered? The walls are too thin here to put her up for another night.

The aroma of freshly brewed coffee filled his nostrils. Returning to the kitchen, he poured a cup. He retreated to the lemon-colored couch.

Sipping the coffee, he watched the bumper-to-bumper traffic on the bridge, devising a plan. I'll phone Molly and smooth things over, assure her that Dora is not a murderess. His brow knit. Yet, how sure am I?

"Here are your pajamas, I didn't use them."

Grayson jumped, turning to see Dora standing completely dressed in the doorway.

Did she sleep in those clothes,? he wondered. "What did you sleep in?"

Dora stared at her navy pumps. I'm embarrassed to tell you."

"Would you like a cup of coffee?" he asked.

"With cream and sugar, please. I can't drink it black."

She followed him into the small kitchen. "Say when," he instructed pouring cream.

The hot liquid turned a light caramel color. Grayson turned the empty pitcher over. "You didn't say when."

"Oh, that's enough, thank you. Her hand trembled holding the cup.

"This is the way I like it."

She followed him back into the living room, moaning, "I just don't know what I'm going to do?"

"I promised you, I will speak to Molly."

"Do you think she'll let me stay at her house again?" Dora's voice sounded childlike. "Everything was perfect until she found out I fibbed."

"Now, now, Grayson patted her shoulder. I have an errand to go on. I promised Bunny I'd take care of her dog while she's away."

"Is Bunny going somewhere?" Dora asked. "If you hadn't come home last night, I was ready to ask if I could stay with her. In spite of her dirty poetry, I think she has a kind heart."

"Bunny is leaving for South America today."

"Maybe I should go some place too?" Do you think Bunny would like a traveling companion?"

"No, not now, you stay put, Dora until I return, then I'll contact Molly."

"I know you'll patch things up?" Dora half smiled. "She'listen to you."

- 29 -

Grayson rode the elevator down to the basement. His silver compact waited in the parking stall. He turned the key in the ignition, smiling, as the engine purred.

Driving down Marina Street, he passed the park already crowded with dog walkers and kite enthusiasts. He gazed at the threatening fog layer lurking near the Golden Gate Bridge. We're going to be socked in before long, he thought.

Turning left, he took a short-cut through the Presidio. Nice, he reflected on the trim green grass bordering the road. On Lake Street, the weather changed. Grayson flicked his windshield wipers on as the fog misted the tinted glass. Strange, he wondered, how one part of The City can be sunny and another dripping. Maybe that's part of San Francisco's charm.

Bunny's pink colonial loomed in sight. There was ample space to park directly in front. He strode up the brick walkway, casually petting one of the cement lions on each side of the entrance. He wondered, did Donald Palmcroft's influence prompt these beasts guarding the front door?

"What do you think of this dress?" Bunny asked without saying hello.

Scanning the strapless evening gown, Grayson stammered, "Very nice." My God, she's almost topless in that. He regained his composure. "Are we having a fashion show?"

"Don't be cute, Gray, I'm trying to get my wardrobe together. Come on in."

"Where's the pooch?" he asked, blinking at the decor in the living room. "Is your favorite color shocking pink, Bunny?"

"How did you guess," she plopped on the couch. "Heartly, Heartly," she called. "He'll come down in a minute. You know I think he senses I'm leaving. Dogs are smart that way."

Heartly bounded down the pink carpeted stairs. Seeing Grayson, he froze, his tail quivering under his hind legs.

"I think he likes you. Let him sniff you. Talk to him."

"Hello Heartly, come over here, boy."

Trembling, he stared at Grayson. He guarded his small area of carpet, emitting feeble growls.

"Just sit down," Bunny advised. "Let him come to you."

Grayson sat on a printed pink settee. He studied the dog. "Does he always shake like that?"

Bunny ignored his question. "See that mark on his side. It's shaped just like a heart. That's why I named him Heartly."

"Well I wish he was more friendly," Grayson said, noting Heartly hadn't moved an inch.

Bunny clapped her hands, calling. "Come on Heartly, be nice to Gray. I'll leave you boys to get acquainted. I must finish my packing."

Bunny sprinted up the stairs. Halfway to the top, she leaned over the rail, and shouted. "The dog food is in the kitchen cabinet. He also has a sweater and raincoat hanging in the hall closet."

"O.K., But he still won't come to me."

All the appliances in the kitchen were a sparkling pink. Were they brand new, Grayson wondered, or did Bunny ever use any of them?

The dog food cans were stacked in a lower cupboard. Grayson loaded them into a paper bag. Leaving the bag in the kitchen, he walked into the hall.

Opening the closet door, he spotted the plastic plaid raincoat hanging above a large hamper. Maybe the sweaters are in here, he thought, opening the hamper.

A blue canvas bag laid on top. There were leather initials "D. P.."

"Donald Palmcroft," Grayson gasped. He unzipped the bag. Under some clothing was a black wallet. Grayson looked inside to see credit cards, a driver's license all with the name, Donald Palmcroft. His fingers gripped something hard and sharp. He drew out a large blood-stained knife. "I see we both like to rummage through hampers." he said surprised. Bunny stood in the doorway.

Grayson's mouth gaped open staring at her black wig.

"Oh this," she brushed the black hair. "Ricardo likes brunettes.

Come into the living room, Gray. Bring the bag if you want." Grayson followed her, carrying the bag. Seating erect on a pink chair, he stared out her speechless.

"Would you care for a drink before I confess?"

Grayson nodded.

She placed a brandy on the coffee table in front of him. "Here's to Donald," she toasted, raising the snifter to her lips. She put the drink down without sipping it.

"You?" Grayson blurted, regaining his voice.

"Drink up."

Grayson took a large gulp. He swallowed. "Go ahead, tell me about this?"

"Donald Palmcroft killed poor Charlie. I hired him for a considerable amount of money. That's one thing, Donald was never cheap. We got away with it because nobody suspected or cared. Charlie was such a bastard. If only Donald hadn't gotten guilt feelings. Hell, two years later he gets a conscience, confessing everything to Darla. You know what her wonderful advice was, blackmail."

"Darla was blackmailing you?"

"She intended to bleed me of all Charlie's money.,"

Grayson finished his drink.

Cupping her chin, Bunny watched him. "I tried to reason with her, but she was so stubborn. Can you believe she wanted half of Charlie's estate.

Where would that leave me? I'd end up a bag lady. I visited her after we had our poetry meeting."

Grayson held his glass. "I need another one."

She poured the liquid, filling the snifter. "I tried the door before ringing the bell. It was open and I walked right into her bedroom. There she was lounging on her bed as naked as a jaybird. She was so busy reading her fan mail, she didn't even look up. 'Come in sweetheart, she said.' The little bitch thought I was Donald."

Of course, I was wearing this," Bunny pointed to her wig. Those dumb glasses she was wearing are only good for close-up vision. I went right at her. For her size, she put up one hell of a fight. She grabbed my jacket and ripped the 'P' right off. That little slut chased me out on the balcony. She should have known better, because one little push and down went Darla. I didn't even have to use my knife."

"What about Flora?" Grayson asked, taking out a handkerchief and wiping his forehead. "Awfully hot in here."

Bunny grinned. "You drank too much, Gray. As for Flora, that was a mistake. Their front door was open, so I walked in and heard her blabbing on the phone. She claimed to know who killed Darla. I thought Donald blabbed to her too." She shrugged. "Those women should remember to lock their front doors. After all he was confessing to everyone. I learned one thing, Gray, when you hire someone you should look for a professional.

It's like contracting a plumber to fix a leak, or an electrician for wiring."

Grayson gulped the last of his drink.

"It's all his fault. What a wimp. He was going to ruin me. I had to stop him and I did. I stabbed him with the same knife I finished Flora with."

Grayson moaned. "Why poor Flora?"

"You know I feel kind of bad about that. It's lucky Dora wasn't home.

I'd have to kill her, too. Gray, you can understand the predicament I was in. What other choice did I have?"

Does she want my sympathy? Grayson wondered.

"That Donald, he grabbed my jacket, and wouldn't let go. I didn't think he'd ever die. I had to keep stabbing him. It took all my strength.

Guess I was too exhausted to notice the torn lining. I'm sure glad you took it. I owe you one Gray, for not telling Dusty."

"Worst mistake I ever made," Grayson mumbled under his breath.

Bunny continued. "I nicked myself a little with the knife. When you told me the police took blood samples, I figured it's only a matter of time before they trace it to me. I lied about Heartly nipping me. Heartly would never bite anyone, would you, sweetie?" Bunny stroked his smooth white coat.

Squirming, Grayson watched the dog's dark brown eyes staring at him. His upper lip curled to expose sharp tiny teeth.

"Why are you telling me all this?" Grayson asked. "Aren't you afraid I'll tell the police, or..." The color drained from his face. "Am I your next victim?"

"Drink up, Gray, It'll be too late to fink on me. I put a sedative in your brandy. You should feel a little woozy about now. You'll be out for about nine hours. Think of me in Rio when you wake up. I can't kill you.

There'd be no one to take care of Heartly. My dog is very important to me.

Grayson's head spun. He tried to focus his eyes. He wondered if they had lead weights forcing them shut? He struggled, shifting his position on the couch.

Bunny watched, smiling faintly at his efforts. "Don't fight it.

"Just relax. I've got to finish packing." She reached for the canvas bag.

"But first, I'll just put this away."

Grayson stretched on the couch, asked "How did you get your jacket back?"

Was she in another room, he wondered. Her voice was muffled. "Those twenty-four hour cleaners are really good. They sewed on another 'P while I waited. None of you could tell the difference. In case you ever need a fast cleaning job, you ought to try them. I'll leave their card on the coffee table."

Grayson tried to move his lips, but his voice wouldn't cooperate.

What had she put in that brandy?

He tried to sit up, but his body was too heavy. Dozing, he heard Bunny's off key rendition of "I Did It My Way."

"Help" he tried to mouth the word, but no sound came.

- 30 -

"Where is he?" Dora muttered, pacing back and forth. He should have returned hours ago. All he had to do was pick up that dog. He knew I was waiting.

Why didn't he ask me to go with him? I would have liked to visit Bunny. She has such progressive ideas except, of course, designing those dumb jackets.

On impulse Dora grabbed the phone. Her fingers begin to press Molly's number. She hesitated before pushing the last digit, reconsidered and hung the receiver up.

Retreating to the couch, she sat staring vacantly out the window. "Oh dear," she moaned, wondering if she should try Molly again. There was so much she wanted to know. How were the cats faring? Was Lord Byron eating? But What if Molly hung-up and refused to talk? Better wait until Grayson comes back. Molly will listen to him.

I don't want to stay her another night, she thought. Maybe I'm old-fashioned, but it just doesn't look right for an unmarried woman to stay with a single, unrelated man.

Rummaging through her over-stuffed purse, she pulled out her car keys.

She dangled the keys. Should I take a drive? It would help consume the long afternoon, besides the tissue box was empty. I could go to a drugstore and buy a couple of boxes for Grayson.

She peered out the window. Thick fog veiled the downtown buildings.

It doesn't look too inviting, but I'll go stir crazy if I stay here.

Clutching her keys, she left the condo. Grayson would surely be back when she returned.

Driving down the narrow street, she passed Coit Tower. Maybe, I'll stop and go inside with the tourists. She circled the block looking for a space large enough for the Land Rover.

Finding none, she decided, No, I'll drive down toward the Marina and find a pharmacy.

She maneuvered the Land Rover down the hill. Reaching the Marina, she slowed down to admire yachts moored in the harbor. The bay sure looks choppy, not a good day for a boat ride.

A blanket of fog hid the towers on the Golden Gate Bridge. The mist thickened on the windshield distorting her vision. Dora switch the wipers on.

Turning on Presidio Avenue, she spotted a small pharmacy on the corner. Good, there was a large space right in front.

She sat in the car for a moment, listening to the fog horns.

Looking up at the gray sky, she visualized Donald's face looking down at her. Tears slid down her cheek. Using her palm, she wiped them.

"You must have a terrible cold," the pharmacist said, stuffing twelve boxes of tissues in a large plastic bag. "The cold remedies and cough syrup are on that shelf." He pointed toward an aisle.

Dora opened the bag and drew out a tissue to wipe her eyes. "No cold," she sobbed.

"An allergy then?" the pharmacist persisted.

Dora didn't answer. Fastening the seat belt in the Land Rover, she placed one of the boxes beside her. Bunny's house can't be far. Her brow knit, contemplating going there uninvited. Of course, I won't go in. I'll only look to see if Grayson's car is still parked there.

Passing the colonial, she noticed the silver compact in front. She reflected, I'll park across the street and wait. He should be leaving soon.

A few minutes passed before a taxi drove up, parking behind Grayson's car. The driver emerged and walked up to the pink colonial's front door.

He rang the bell.

Bunny appeared. She handed the driver a large suitcase. Goodness, Dora thought, doesn't she look nice all dressed up.

Leaning out of the window, Dora watched Bunny follow the driver to the cab. She jumped in the back seat while the man shoved the suitcase in the trunk.

Dora waved. "Bunny, Bunny," she shouted. Oh dear, she doesn't hear me. Smiling, Dora edged out of the Land Rover to greet Bunny. Her smile faded as the cab sped away.

What is Grayson still doing in there? She wondered. I'll wait a couple of minutes, he's bound to come out. Bunny sure has a pretty garden, she thought, admiring a patch of pink carnations. It's chilly out here. She wrapped her coat tighter around her plump frame.

This is ridiculous, I can't stand around here forever. I'll just go and ring the bell. She pressed the doorbell. There was barking, but no one answered. She knocked, first with her fist and then tapped her keys on the wood. "Grayson, Grayson, it's me," she called.

Why doesn't he answer? Maybe if I walk around and peek through that window, I'll find out what's going on. Standing on her tiptoes, she peeked in.

"What in the world?" she uttered, spotting Grayson lying on the couch.

A small white dog perched on his chest. She tapped her keys against the glass. The dog barred his teeth, growling at her. "Bad dog," Dora admonished, wagging her finger at the dog. She trudged back to the front of the house. Exasperated, she gripped the brass door knob. "My goodness," she murmured, as the door swung open. "I thought I was the only one who didn't lock doors."

Rushing into the living room, Dora cried, "Grayson, Grayson." She shook his shoulders, pleading "Please wake up."

The little dog danced around her yipping. Dora sobbed, thinking maybe he's dead.

She leaned over him, sobbing. "Why don't you wake up?" Dumping the contents of her purse on the pink carpet, she searched for a mirror. I could hold it under his nose and see if he's breathing.

Darn it, No mirror. Ah, but his chest is moving. He is breathing.

"Why don't you wake up?" She picked up a tissue from the carpet and dabbed her eyes, wondering what to do?

She rushed into the kitchen. Maybe if she poured some cold water over his limp body. A pink wall phone caught her eye.

I must get help, she thought, dialing 9ll. "Police, this is an emergency!"

- 31 -

Heartly hid in the kitchen as Dora opened the door. Dusty Merkel accompanied by two officers entered.

"Oh, I'm so glad you're here," Dora said, leading them into the living room.

"What's all that on the rug?" one of the officers asked.

Blushing, Dora admitted, "It's just stuff from my purse. I'll pick it up."

"There he is on the couch."

Dusty waved a vial under Grayson's nostrils. "This should bring him around."

"Thank God, he's alive," Dora uttered, to the two officers standing beside her. "Look his eye lids are fluttering."

"Grayson Crown, Grayson Crown," Dusty repeated.

Grayson's lips quivered, as he tried to mouth words.

"Come on, we're listening," Dusty encouraged.

"Look in bag. Bunny killed."

"That's silly," Dora announced. "I just saw Bunny, she looked very well."

"Shhhhh, Miss Stromboli," one of the officers said. "He's trying to tell us something."

"Bag," Grayson mumbled, "Look in closet."

"That's Donald's!" Dora exclaimed, as one of the officers carried the canvas bag in.

"Look at this." The policeman removed the blood-stained knife.

Straining, Grayson hoisted himself to a sitting position. "Bunny killed them all. She confessed." He groaned.

Dora sobbed, watching him fall back on the couch.

"He's out again," Dusty said.

"Oh, it's all making sense now. Bunny killed my Donald." Her fingers fumbled, reaching for a tissue from the carpet.

"Get an ambulance," Dusty instructed. "Where is Bunny Masterson?"

Dora blew her nose before replying. "She's on her way to Rio.

Grayson was going to take care of her dog." She pointed to Heartly peeking out from the kitchen.

"Radio one of the squad cars. We must pick up this Masterson woman."

Dora gazed at the pink rosebud clock on the mantel. "It's too late," she moaned. "Her plane was 'spose to leave at six. It's five after now."

She stared at the ceiling. "She's up in the sky now, getting away with murder."

"You evidently didn't listen to the weather report," Dusty said. "The airport is socked in. No planes will take off until this fog lifts."

"Really," Dora still looked doubtful.

"Don't worry, Maam, she'll be stuck at the airport for hours. I'll take care of her, personally."

Sirens screamed. Gazing out the window, Dora saw the ambulance's flashing lights.

Two attendants hoisted Grayson on a gurney.

Dora touched his hand. "He looks so pale."

"He'll be all right," Dusty reassured her.

As Grayson rolled past him, Dusty saluted. "You have more guts than I gave you credit for."

- 32 -

Perched on a tall leather bar stool, Bunny sipped her Vodka. She gazed out the window at the thick blanket of grayness. Damn, she thought, wouldn't it ever lift? Glancing at the clock behind the bar, she frowned.

It's after six already, I should be on my way by now.

Why worry? Those drops were strong. Grayson would be unconscious for hours unable to tell anyone of her whereabouts. Relax, I'm safe. The plane has to take off soon. They don't ground planes long. Yeah, she rationalized, people would get too upset. They'd take buses. The airlines would lose a lot of money.

Gazing at the bartender, she thought he's kinda' cute. Did he just wink at me? There's no time to flirt now. She concentrated on Rio. It will be lovely there this time of year.

She rested her hand by her drink, admiring her well-manucured nails.

What was that polish called? Scarlet Neon something? It would probably have a different name in Rio.

She twisted the diamond band off her fourth finger. Wrapping the ring in a cocktail napkin, she carefully deposited it into the zippered compartment in her purse. It would never do to meet Ricardo wearing Charlie's wedding band. If I hadn't been in such a rush, I could have sold it. That diamond is worth a couple of thousand at least. Pulling a cigarette out, she placed it between her full lips. Magnet-like, it drew the curly-haired bartender. Suddenly, he was standing in front of her.

"Let me," he offered lighting a match.

"Thank you," she said, taking a deep drag. She blew the smoke out slowly, eying the bartender. He placed a clean ashtray on the bar.

She took a sip of her drink. "Have you heard any news about when the planes will take off?" she asked.

"They'll announce it over the P.A.. "Just stay here, you'll hear it, Miss."

Bunny smiled. How complementary, he called me Miss.

"Hey Barkeep," a voice from the other end of the bar called, "How about some service down here?"

Bunny stared down at her half-full glass, thinking. If it wasn't for that Donald Palmcroft, I could have stayed in San Francisco. Why did I get mixed up with that wimp? I should have hired professionals to take care of Charlie. There would be no repercussions that way. A hired gun is ethical, and wouldn't have considered blackmail. They're business like, just like plumbers. You pay them and they fix the problem. That's it, no emotional involvement and no guilty conscience. Damn Donald, telling everyone.

"Blabbermouth," she muttered.

"Did you say something?" a deep voice asked.

Turning, she saw a man with handsome rugged features sitting on the bar stool to her right.

"I was just wondering when the planes are going to take off," she said, fluttering her eyelids.

"Where are you bound to?" he asked.

"Rio, I'm taking a little vacation." He's good looking, she thought as his deep blue eyes met hers.

"Rio's nice at this time of year." He volunteered, "I'm on my way to New York. Convention," he explained, if that pea-soup ever clears."

"Oh," Bunny finished the rest of her drink.

"I'll only be gone about three days."

The bartender approached. Noticing Bunny's empty glass, he asked, "Can I get you another one, Miss?"

Bunny nodded. "Vodka on the rocks,. Don't forget the lime twist."

He smiled and leaning over, whispered, "Sexy Mama."

"Fresh," she snapped.

Ignoring his lingering stare, she turned to the man on her right. "I guess we're stuck here for a while." She squashed her cigarette as the bartender replaced her drink.

"Let me take care of that," the man offered. "Another Scotch for me," he told the bartender.

Raising her glass, Bunny said, "Here's to you."

"My name is Richard Fair."

"I'm Bunny Masterson. What time was your plane scheduled to take off?" She drew out another cigarette.

"I've been waiting for about two hours." His arm extended, displaying a gold lighter. The flame touched the end of her cigarette as she inhaled.

"Thank you, all this waiting is nerve wracking."

"Yeah, the worst of it is that I have season tickets for the 49'ers.

Won't be able to go Sunday."

"Oh, I adore football," Bunny lied.

"Maybe we can go to a game when you return to The City?"

"That would be nice."

Before Richard answered, Bunny felt a tap on her shoulder.

She turned to face Dusty Merkel.

"Bunny Masterson?" Dusty Merkel inquired.

"Why, Detective Merkel," Bunny smiled. "How nice to see you again."

"You're under arrest, Mrs. Masterson, for suspicion of murder."

"You must be kidding!" Bunny exclaimed. Two blue-coated officers approached.

"Read her rights," Dusty instructed one of them.

Bunny's mouth gaped open listening to his monotone voice. She grasped Richard's arm. "There must be some mistake."

"Let's go, Miss Masterson. You will come quietly, we don't want any trouble."

"Oh dear," she moaned. "Goodbye Richard, it was nice meeting you."

"Take this, we may meet again," he answered, placing a business card in her hand.

Walking out, Bunny read the card: "Richard Fair, Attorney at Law, specializing in criminal law."

- Epilogue -

"And then what happened?" Molly asked, peering at Grayson stretched out on the lemon-colored couch.

He pulled back the green afghan, allowing Heartly to snuggle against his chest. "When Bunny confessed to hiring Donald Palmcroft to kill Charlie, she also admitted to pushing Darla off the balcony and stabbing Flora and Donald. She claimed just cause."

"What do you think they'll do to her?" Nancy asked, slicing a chocolate cheesecake.

"Probably incarcerate her for a long time," Grayson replied, allowing Heartly to lick his hand.

"She should be," Dora said, emphatically.

Grayson gazed out the window at the Bay Bridge. It looked close enough to touch. The fog had dissipated leaving a lazy blue sky.

"Have some cheesecake," Nancy interrupted his thoughts.

Propping his head on an overstuffed pillow, he reached for the plate.

He took a large bite. "Delicious cake, Molly."

Heartly pawed Grayson. His tongue hanging out.

"Don't let the dog eat it," Dora advised. "Chocolate isn't 'spose to be good for them."

Stroking Heartly, Grayson asked. "Would one of you ladies go into the kitchen. There's a box of dog biscuits on the counter."

"I'll go," Molly volunteered.

"I hear Bunny's attorney, Richard Fair, is very capable, Nancy said.

Molly handed Grayson the dog biscuits. Under her arm she carried a large cardboard box. "I've got a present for everyone. It's from my daughter-in-law, Pepper. She said to share it with you."

Nancy helped remove the packing. "Dermisqueeze," she announced.

"There must be five hundred tubes in here."

"Well, Pepper told me, she sent a year's supply. Do any of you have any painful corns?" She asked, passing the box around as if it was a plate of hors d'oeuvres. "Help yourself."

Dora reached for a tube. "I don't have any now, but who knows?"

"None for me, thank you," Nancy said.

"Perhaps you can donate what's left to some charity?" Grayson suggested.

"Molly wants me to move in with her permanently." Dora said, her eyes twinkling. "That big old Victorian is much too big for me. I've decided to sell it."

"Yes," Molly shoved the Dermasqueeze carton in a corner. "It will be wonderful having Dora and her cats share my house. I've gotten to like Charlotte, Elizabeth, and the Little Lord a lot."

"It's Emily," Dora corrected.

Nancy's brow knit, "Now that everything is settled, I still don't understand what happened to Molly's and my 'Power Of Poetry' jackets?"

Dora squirmed, her face turning a deep rose. "That was me."

"You!" All eyes focused on her.

Dora swallowed and cleared her throat. "Those jackets were horrible, I drowned them in the lake at Golden Gate Park."

"You threw our jackets away?" Nancy repeated.

"Mine, too! They weren't very becoming. At our age, we looked stupid in those things."

"I agree," Molly wrapped her arm around Dora's shoulder.

"Women over sixty shouldn't wear motorcycle jackets."

- end -

About the Author

Barbara J. Less has written over a hundred short stories. Most of them have been published in literary magazines. She has also written articles about her family of Italian Greyhounds. These have been published in Dog World, Dog Fancy and other dog magazines.

A few years ago one of her stories, Live Entertainment won first prize in a national contest.

She also has appeared on local television reading her stories.

www.ingramcontent.com/pod-product-compliance
Ingram Content Group UK Ltd.
Pitfield, Milton Keynes, MK11 3LW, UK
UKHW040015200726
13854UKWH00001B/224

9 780759 659292